DEMON HUNTER

DEMON GUARDIANS
BOOK 3

TERRY SPEAR

PUBLISHED BY:

Wilde Ink Publishing

Demon Hunter

Copyright © 2018 by Terry Spear

Cover Copyright by Terry Spear

Discover more about Terry Spear at:

http://www.terryspear.com/

Print ISBN: 978-1-63311-033-5

Ebook ISBN: 978-1-63311-032-8

Thanks to Janice Bolick, who loves my stories and follows me on Goodreads! May you have the best of times always!

BLURB FOR DEMON HUNTER:

Returning to the demon world is dangerous, but they're willing to risk it to find family.

Hunter is half a Matusa demon, determined to help his human-raised demon friends return to the demon world to find their families. And to help Alana learn a way to keep portals from pulling her to them, and getting herself into all kinds of trouble. Not that she can't handle some of the trouble on her own. She's a half demon too, and half witch. Jared is looking for his parents. Celeste is looking for hers. Samson is there to protect Alana, though Hunter keeps reminding him Alana is his to protect.

It was a simple mission, but nothing for the demon guardians is ever simple. Between dealing with a demon who is organizing demon hunters—who go after Hunter and his friends, a major train wreck, and all sorts of havoc, it's no wonder the demon gate guardians end up calling in reinforcements this time.

As long as Hunter can get Alana to agree to be his mate, he can save the world. Alana will never give up her hot demon, but she believes he should work a little harder to prove he is the one for her. And he's not going to give up trying to convince her either. But they still have one little problem: staying alive long enough to do it.

Ready for a fun-filled, cliff-hanging adventure? Check out Demon Hunter!

1

When other seniors in high school were thinking about spring break and all the trouble they could get into south of the border, Alana and her demon friends were planning the hot-spot destination of Seplichus, the demon world—and the search for other demons.

Specifically, their friend Celeste's kin—her summoner parents having been murdered by a Matusa when she was just three years old, so she didn't know who her real parents were—Jared's parents, Alana's father, and Hunter's half-brother.

They could go to the Hall of Records in three more days and hopefully locate everyone they needed.

"Omigod, he is the hottest thing ever," a blond-haired girl said to another, eyeing Hunter as he made another boy move from his seat in Alana's English class so he could sit next to Alana and watch over her.

Alana rolled her eyes at him. *She* was a total demon magnet because of her Kubiteron demon kind, but Hunter was a total human girl magnet. He was a half-Matusa demon, one of the evil kind, though Hunter's human half tempered his demon half.

Alana couldn't believe how bold the girls were when they were nearby, making sure he heard just how interested they were in him. Alana couldn't deny the attraction she had for him and the annoyance she felt for him. Yet she loved working with him when she didn't want to kill him. He was a Matusa, after all, and that meant he was arrogant and stubborn to a fault.

Well-muscled because of his martial arts training to fight the evil ones and send them back to their world, he was totally hot. He was dark-haired and dark-eyed, just like she liked guys, his hair shaggy, bad-boy look, perfect.

It didn't matter one iota that Hunter stuck close to Alana as much as he could, worried about her being pulled to an opening demon portal. If the human girls could do neat tricks like that, maybe *they* could have garnered his interest.

He glanced at her and gave her a small smile. She was certain it was because he wanted her to know she was lucky to have him....according to the human girls. Or maybe he was just amused that they were interested in him, and it annoyed her. Though she was trying not to let it show.

Before she could say something to wipe that smug smile off his face—Indigo moved in between them. The ghostly Matusa demon was torn between wanting to haunt the students in the classroom that she was in *or* that Celeste Sweetwater was in—another one of their demon friends thrown together with them due to the strange events of the past year—and their group was fast becoming a melting pot of demon guardians.

Their purpose: keep the Matusa demons from entering Earth world and returning any of the demons that people summoned into their world to Seplichus.

Hunter growled low under his breath, "Get lost, Matusa."

Hunter didn't like that any other demon would try to come between him and Alana. Even if the demon was merely a ghost. But Indigo was a *full* Matusa demon, and he felt that Alana *was* his. So did Hunter, despite being only half demon.

"Admit it," Alana whispered to Hunter, "he's one of us now. We would miss him if he wasn't on our team."

Hunter grunted.

Indigo had helped them so many times when facing the danger of the Matusa demons, they really owed him their lives.

At the end of the period, the teacher gave out their reading assignments. When they left the class, Jared rushed to meet them at their lockers. Jared had been fighting demons with Hunter for a number of years already. His dark hair was wind-blown, his amber eyes narrowed, and he was trying to catch his breath.

Jared was the computer geek of the bunch, always coming up with cool new gadgets to help them in their quest. "Have I mentioned how dumb it is for us to return to high school?"

"Daily," Hunter said, exchanging books at his wall locker.

"Yeah, well"—Jared waved his demon monitor tracker, the size of a cell phone at him—"my tracker picked up activity at the Jiffy Ice Cream Shop. How are we going to leave the school to check it out?"

"What kind of demon?" Hunter asked, frowning.

A blond-haired girl and her dark-haired girlfriend moved closer and said, "Oooh, are you into summoning demons?"

Jared tucked his demon tracker II device into his pocket, while Alana and Hunter scowled at the girls.

"You mean, like a video game?" Hunter asked, growling a little.

They couldn't believe how the Matusa demons were infiltrating their world, via being summoned. Once one was here, he'd encourage more summonings. No one could ever be sure what kind of demon they summoned either, until they were there. Strictly humans didn't know there was a grand difference between demon kind.

To some though, it was just a game. They didn't really believe messing with summoning spells would bring any demon to their world. If they called a Matusa, they would be dead before they realized summoning demons wasn't a game.

The girl pulled some books out of the locker near Hunter's. "Summoning demons in a video game? Of course not. We heard you talking before about demons, and we wondered if you're into that role-playing game."

"What role-playing game?" Hunter sounded annoyed but concerned also.

Even if it was some lame game they were playing, they always had to take any mention of demons seriously.

Alana was worried too. Summoning demons could be really bad news for everyone. They couldn't dismiss that the girls might be talking about something that was for real.

Any hint of demon summoning activity and the demon guardians were on it. They had to be. They owed it to their kind—both on this side and in Seplichus, the demon world. The humans, or at least most of them, were clueless.

"Well, it's a secret, so if you're not into demons," the blond said, shrugging.

"Oh, we're *very* much into demons," Jared said, who was a full Elantus demon, no human blood at all. "What is the game all about?"

TONIGHT, they had to scope out the extra-curricular activities of the self-professed demon hunters, but for now, Hunter and Jared slipped out of school to check on the demon at the ice cream shop, while Alana protested that she wanted to come also. But *she* had to graduate from high school.

Hunter and Jared had already graduated, had diplomas, and were just pretending to need their senior year at Alana's high school to watch over her. Celeste was in the same boat as Alana, needing another year of high school to earn her diploma. She was taking another class for now, though she was a couple of years older them. Moving from one school to another because of moving from one foster family to another had been the problem for her. And, well, skipping school.

With a stern word to Samson, Alana's self-proclaimed gate guardian guard—Hunter had told him to watch over her at all costs. Alana was supposed to be a gate guardian, and Samson, as a Samuria demon, claimed to be her guard and her intended mate, which neither Alana nor Hunter bought into. Samson wasn't even of this world, so he definitely didn't need any human schooling, but he sure was good at it, Hunter had to admit.

Hunter hoped Alana would stay put. He didn't trust her one little bit. Once he'd assured himself that she wasn't going anywhere —the demon having already being summoned, apparently, so there would be no portal opening that would pull Alana's astral form to it —he and Jared took off for the ice cream shop.

"Are you certain your demon tracker is accurately showing the demon type?" Hunter asked Jared.

"Yeah, Celeste's kind of demon. A Camaran demon."

"Then it's probably her signature you're seeing. Did you try to reach Celeste on her cell phone and make sure she's not skipping classes again?"

"Yes, and she must have her cell phone turned off. I haven't been able to get ahold of her."

"But she, or whoever the Camaran demon is, is still at the ice cream shop."

Jared glanced down at the tracker that he had built himself. He was a whiz at stuff like that. "Yeah."

"What about tracking Celeste at school?"

"She hides her demon aura. So I don't know if she's at school or not. She kind of blinks on and off sometimes. I swear it's to annoy me."

Hunter smiled. Demon types were like that.

"I see Alana's Kubiteron demon type in class, Samson's Samuria signature, sitting next to her. Then you and me in your vehicle driving—" Jared paused as he glanced at the shop as they passed it by. "Hey, Hunter, you just passed the ice cream shop."

"Matusa demon is straight ahead."

"Uh...wait, my demon tracker shows that's a Camaran. How did he, oh, he's running."

"He must be one of the kinds who can mask his demon type. For a moment, he shed his Camaran masking, and I saw his true demon type."

"Does he know we're following him?"

"I don't think so. He has to have been here a while if he didn't just come through a portal or Alana would have been pulled to it."

Suddenly, the demon whipped around, stared hard at Hunter, then turned his attention to Jared, and back to Hunter. And grinned.

"Hold on tight. We're in for trouble," Hunter said, trying to make a corner, the car's tires squealing, before the Matusa blasted them out of existence.

2

S amson poked at Alana, and though she felt him trying to get her attention, she was long gone. At least, she was astral traveling again, her body in another place, but just as real as the one in the classroom she'd left behind.

She'd promised Hunter she'd stay put. But she knew it didn't mean a whole lot. Not when her demon powers, or maybe it had something to do with her witch's half, decided otherwise for her. At least, this time she wasn't in a shower before she was pulled from her body, leaving a shell of herself behind.

Suddenly, she was facing one pissed off Matusa demon, who gaped at her unexpected appearance. She saw Hunter and Jared in Hunter's pickup tear off down a side street two blocks past the ice cream shop. Jared hadn't said the demon was a Matusa. Had they lied to her so she didn't insist on coming along?

Demon types were notorious liars.

The Matusa straightened a little, and she expected him to say the same old malarkey, "You're mine, Kubiteron."

It was getting to be old hat, and she truly wished they would get a new come-on line. Not that she would buy it any more than she would agree to become a Matusa's mate, just because they liked Kubiteron demons above all others.

"What have we here?" the demon said instead, as if he didn't know. Or maybe he recognized she wasn't all here.

Although with recent changes, she truly was all there. It was her other half, still sitting in the classroom, that was left in limbo. She envisioned the school bell ringing for the class to let out, and Samson guiding her out of the room, while he frantically called on Hunter to let him know Alana wasn't all there.

"Did someone summon you?" She folded her arms, trying to act all innocent as if she'd been summoned also, and maybe he could be her protector. *As if.*

Matusa demons were the strongest of all demons and fighting him head-on was not a viable option for her. Hunter could manage with a good fight, but not her.

She just had to stall the Matusa long enough for Jared to tell Hunter that he was seeing two Kubiterons on his tracker device. One Kubiteron standing in front of the Matusa here, and one at the school with Samson. Samson would probably be calling him at the same time. Any moment, Hunter would be wheeling around the corner in rescue mode.

She didn't hear any sign of him. And that totally annoyed her. What good was he at being her all-protective, hot, half-Matusa demon boyfriend if he wasn't here to protect her?

"Come with me." Matusa stalked toward her.

She backed up. This was where the trouble came in. She couldn't return to her human form back at school. She still didn't have any control over that aspect of astral traveling. At least not yet. Before, if he tried to grab her, his hand would go right through her. But now? He would grab her and haul her right out of here.

"Don't be afraid, little one." His eyes were dark brown like Hunter's, his hair dark brown, the same shaggy length, only he was older, maybe in his late twenties, but he was muscular like Hunter, who, when he wasn't taking classes with her, was practicing swords-manship and martial arts.

Anything to keep in shape to take down the demons who entered Earth world with the intention of ruling here.

"Where is your summoner?" the Matusa asked, still moving forward, and she continued to move backward toward the street where Hunter had disappeared.

"Anytime would be a good time to make your appearance, Hunter," she told him telepathically. She'd learned early on she could communicate with him in that manner, only he couldn't telepathi-cally communicate with her back. So it was always a one-sided conversation. If he didn't hear her because he was too far away, she wouldn't have a clue.

The Matusa was walking cautiously as if afraid she would bolt. As tall as he was, he would catch up to her easily if she took off running. Instead, she held his sympathetic gaze with a feigned, frightened one of her own. That was the only way to make him believe he had the upper hand. Well, more so than he already did.

Though she did have some demon and witch's tricks up her sleeve.

"My summoner is dead." Though in truth, she was born to a human mother, who was also a witch, and was perfectly alive, and ghostbusting, as was her job.

The Matusa smiled. It was a smile borne of intrigue and desire. She would be the Matusa's. No one would stand in his way.

No one would if Hunter didn't get his butt back here and protect her.

Well, there was only one thing for her to do. And it wasn't anything she ever wished to do. Nor was it something she should do.

She thought if she could draw him into a portal into the demon world, and she could turn around and reenter Earth world fast enough, she would close the portal, and he would be back where he belonged. It was great that, since she and Hunter were half demons, they could open portals into the demon world, but that full demons, even like Jared and the rest of their guardian team, couldn't.

Which meant any full demon would be stuck back in their world unless someone summoned him here. And if it was a Matusa? They killed their summoners. Simple as that.

Her plan was sound as long as: She could draw him into the portal. He didn't grab her in the demon world before she left there. Someone else didn't grab her. Or something else happened that she hadn't even thought of.

In other words, there were some holes in her otherwise brilliant plan.

"Don't...be...afraid," the Matusa said, his voice dark and appealing, like Hunter's was.

All Matusa had that dark appealing voice down pat. It was probably similar to the sweetness of the siren's lure, the mermaid's, if they existed. Or a vampire's gaze and commanding voice, if they existed.

She was trying really hard not to grind her teeth, annoyed with Hunter to the max.

"Okay, Hunter, if you're not here in sixty seconds, I've got to do this myself."

She didn't have time to wait sixty seconds. The demon charged after her, and she dove down the street where she'd seen Hunter's truck disappear.

It was now or never.

She was going to kill Hunter if she got herself out of the pickle of a mess she was in, if she lived to do the deed.

HUNTER HATED how much his world turned upside down when Alana was in trouble. First, Jared warned him that there were suddenly two Kubiteron demons, one at school, and one facing off the Matusa, when there was no sign of a portal. That probably meant only one thing. Alana was astral traveling.

Before Hunter could check with Samson, the Samuria called Jared, which was getting to be an annoying habit of his, instead of calling Hunter, the one in charge. Unless Samson was afraid to call Hunter, then that was fine. All lesser demons were to fear the Matusa. It was just the way of things.

"They're both headed down the street we took," Jared said, his voice on edge. He was always calm, almost always, so Hunter knew it was bad news. "He's...he's chasing her. And she's running, but he's going to catch up to her."

"I can't turn around in here." The construction on either side of the street as they'd dug up asphalt while working on water lines precluded that. Hunter was ready to have a meltdown.

"Watch out!" Jared yelled.

A woman pushing a baby stroller was crossing the walk at the stop sign, the same one Hunter wasn't about to stop for so he could get back to Alana in time. He swore the next time he went anywhere that she was going with him. Though it wouldn't have mattered. It was her astral form that was in trouble for now.

He slammed on his brakes, skidding to a stop right before the painted line that indicated cars needed to stop behind it as the woman glowered at him.

"What's happening?" Hunter asked as the mother and her baby reached the sidewalk, and he pulled through the stop sign. He tore around the corner, driving like he was on a racetrack, hoping no cops were in the area.

Jared didn't answer him.

Hunter glanced over at him, right before he turned onto the

street where they'd seen the Matusa. Jared was staring at the monitor, but Hunter knew it wasn't good. "What?"

"He got her."

"Where are they headed now?" They couldn't just vanish. Well, Alana could. If she had control over her astral traveling. She would be right back at school, safe and sound.

"They...aren't headed anywhere. They just...vanished."

"He couldn't have taken her to the demon world," Hunter said, furious.

"Right. Exactly. She had to have taken him. It's the only way."

SEPLICHUS! No way had Alana intended to be pulled into the demon world with the Matusa. It was storming here, on top of everything else, and she was already drenched to the skin.

Alana raised her fingers and cast a levitation spell at the Matusa demon, but she reacted too late. He grabbed her arm and at the same time, she managed to elevate both of them.

Which didn't do her any good.

She set them both down, then tried to jerk her arm free from his steel grip.

"You are so going to hurt when my mate gets hold of you." She hoped her strong declaration would make the Matusa demon pause.

Not that Hunter was her mate, but she hoped that this Matusa might decide she wasn't worth the aggravation. She thought they stayed with their mate until death do us part, but then again, he might very well intend to kill Hunter to have her.

"You," the Matusa said, "are not mated. You have no ring. I am Viton and you are?" His strong grip on her arm never loosened as she wished she could return to her astral form. When she was stuck in the demon world, that made rejoining her physical form more difficult. Impossible, most likely.

"Alana."

"Kubiteron are healers," he said, stalking toward a train station. "They don't do whatever it was that you did back there to get us here."

"Well, for your information, I do. Which means you really don't want to have me around. Where are you taking me?"

"Porto. The storm city. My residence. Where you and I will learn more about each other."

No one was out in the rainstorm, the violent wind blowing it sideways, and lightning flashed overhead.

Alana was soaked, her jeans, her running shoes, her T-shirt, and hair. She swore she stepped in every puddle she could manage, not missing any of them, before they reached the train station. Northwest Station the sign said.

She telepathically communicated her location to Hunter, in case he was anywhere in the vicinity. As if he'd figured out where she was and created a portal to come through and rescue her.

"Delay him," a male voice said in her head.

Her heart nearly stopped, and she tripped, and fell to the wet pavement, yanking her arm free from Viton.

Viton came back for her, but she again used her levitation spell, raising him high as the rusty, red-painted train pulled into the station. The doors opened, and she tossed him inside as he howled revenge. The doors were still open, various demon kinds peering out the window at her. She just hoped another Matusa wouldn't bolt out of the train for her while she held Viton in place. Viton screamed in fury.

Had Hunter telepathically communicated with her? He'd never been able to before. But she had to concentrate on Viton. "Close the blasted doors," she said under her breath.

They finally slid shut and she released Viton, who would have fallen to the floor. He was cursing so loudly, she could hear him over the sound of the train clacking on the metal tracks as he stared at her through the glass door.

He probably wanted to kill her. She never knew how the Matusa would really act. They were deadly. At the same time, they could surprise her.

She heard someone running toward her in the cold rain and turned to see another Matusa rushing toward her.

"I'm leaving here, Hunter. I can't wait for you. Return home! I'm free." She quickly opened the portal and jumped through it. So did the Matusa.

This was *so* not her day.

~

"COME ON, Jared. She's safely back 'home' now," Hunter said.

"When is she ever safe?" Jared asked. "I know it's her calling, that she's a gate guardian, but I wish she had better control over it. Or that we could disable the trigger that makes her astral travel to the open portals so she would no longer feel the pull of them. We have enough work as it is without having to rescue her all the time."

Hunter opened a portal in Seplichus so they could return to their world. As soon as they jumped through it, they found themselves about a mile from where they'd left the truck. They were soaking wet from their journey to the demon world, while it was sunshiny here.

"Okay, so where is she?" Jared asked.

"Hunter!"

"In trouble, it sounds like, if her shrieking my name in my head is any indication."

"She didn't leave the Matusa in Seplichus? Give a girl a job and see what she does with it? Mucks it up!" Jared grumbled, still eyeing the tracker.

"Are you tracking their demon signatures?"

"Yeah, yeah. She's straight ahead, quarter of a mile. Matusa and Kubiteron. Wait. The Kubiteron..."

"What?"

"She's gone. At the school it appears. The Matusa is still straight ahead, just standing there. Probably wondering where Alana just disappeared to."

Hunter shook his head. "Just like *we* always do." He got on his phone. "Samson, is Alana back?"

"Yeah. *Finally.* Text later."

"Okay. We've got to take care of a Matusa." Hunter mentally prepared himself to fight him and hoped, when he opened a portal to send the Matusa back to the demon world, it didn't summon Alana here again. She needed to hurry and finish school so they could tie the knot. At least that way the Matusa demons would leave her alone.

Or...so he hoped.

3

_____

lana had just returned to her human form where Samson had taken her to the cafeteria. She was starving for a large slice of peperoni pizza, when she was pulled back to where Hunter and Jared were standing. The blue-green portal's swirling lights mesmerized her for a minute until she focused on the threat. One older Matusa was tossing a fireball at Hunter. She immediately cast a water barrier protection spell, and the fireball hit the water and sizzled and fizzled out.

"What are you doing here?" Hunter asked, as if he didn't know.

"Not my choice, and if you didn't see what I did, I am protecting you."

Hunter shook his head, but he was raising his hands, and she knew he was trying to give the man a heart attack, like he'd done with other Matusa demons before this.

The portal was beginning to close, and she reopened it. Hunter rushed forth and struck the Matusa in the chest with a hard kick, sending him back into the portal. Alana hurried to close it. "Sheesh, I was about to get some lunch. Can we put a hold on all this until I've eaten?"

Before Hunter could say anything, she vanished and was sitting beside Samson in the lunchroom where he was texting someone. "I'm back." Then she smiled. "You got me a pepperoni pizza."

"You were eyeing it and smiling, before you vanished again, which meant that's what you wanted. I just didn't expect you to leave again so soon. We are meant to be a match."

She let out her breath. "Says you."

"You know I'm the one for you. Admit it."

She had to admit he was cute, blond hair, green eyes, muscular, ready to dish out some punishment to the bad guys—while protecting her.

They saw the girls who had asked them about summoning demons, and the girls smiled at them, but sat at another table.

"Should we join them?" Alana asked.

"I think we're playing with fire here," Samson said.

"They are. They don't know what they're getting into. Come on." When they moved over to the girls' table, Alana asked, "Can we join you?"

"Sure. So, are you coming tonight?"

"Yeah, sure," Alana said.

Samson was picking at his pizza. "Do you ever consider how dangerous it could be—dealing with demons?"

They laughed. "We know just how to deal with them."

Hunter and Jared crossed the floor to join them. Hunter was a little taller than Jared, and more muscular. He looked like he could kick demon butt. Which he could. "We need to talk," Hunter said to Alana.

She smiled at him, raising a brow. Telepathically, she said, *"How in the world were you able to speak to me this time?"*

"You are mine. You should know that by now." Hunter smiled back at her, his look pure evil.

She loved him for it.

"Come on, we need to talk," Hunter said.

She finished her last bite of pizza and intended to go with him, figuring Jared and Samson would butt out, but both of them tagged along.

"So what happened this time?" Samson asked.

"How can you protect the gate guardian if you can't keep her from astral traveling?" Hunter asked him, his tone irritated.

"I *was* protecting her. All right? And I got her favorite pizza for her."

"I saved her life." Hunter was still trying to prove she was better off with him than with Samson.

"Are we really going to that demon meeting tonight?" Jared asked.

"Yeah," Hunter said. "So be prepared for anything."

THAT NIGHT, Hunter, Alana, Jared, and Samson met near where they were supposed to join the demon hunters. Hunter gave them last minute directions. "Be wary of what they're going to do. If they're doing anything illegal, we'll stop them. Otherwise, we just wing it, listen to what they have to say, and agree."

"Or disagree. I'm not just going along with this," Alana said. "It's not that long before we go to Seplichus for spring break, and I don't want them messing up our plans. We learn what we can, do something about it, and we're all set to go to the demon world."

"Which we really shouldn't be doing," Hunter said. *Again.* He did worry about taking her there.

"Does anyone know where Celeste is?" Jared asked.

"Skipping school," Alana and Samson said.

"Who knows where she gets off to," Alana added. "As for Indigo, I felt his icy presence a while back. He might already be at the meeting, trying to listen in on what's being said before we get there."

"Okay, let's go," Hunter said. This was where they belonged:

Earth world, protecting humans. Not traipsing around the demon world looking for family. Though he understood why the others would want to.

Hunter was certain his half-brother would be here in Earth world, but he didn't have any idea where. Would the Hall of Records have information about his dad's other half-human offspring? He'd learned about his father in the Hall of Records, but Hunter hadn't checked to see if he was listed there also. Everyone had to register where they lived. But did they register where half-human offspring lived if they were still in the human world? He doubted it.

Alana took his hand and wrapped it around her waist. "Protect me from the human demon hunters, oh Dark One."

"You laugh, but you could be right about this."

"I know. I hope it's just some foolishness, but we have to be sure."

When they reached the clearing in the woods where the group of "demon hunters" were meeting, they eyed the newcomers with suspicion.

A large fire was glowing, flames licking the chilly air. The trees surrounding them were mostly leafless, just dark branches silhouetted by the fire, the ground covered in a blanket of red, yellow, brown, and orange leaves.

"Okay so we're demon hunters," a brawny kid said, black hair, his dark eyes narrowed as a group of ten kids—other than the ones who had the real demon heritage—met in a wooded area beyond a housing development. "Wait, who said all these guys could join the team?" Yet he looked intrigued that he would have more minions to rule. Especially when he caught sight of Alana. Then his mouth curved up with wicked interest.

Hunter glanced at Alana, her blond hair in curls resting on her shoulders, and if he hadn't known she was a half-Kubiteron demon, he would have thought she was the prettiest girl there anyway. She was smart, good at killing demons, and healing others, and he had to admit that she'd saved his life at great risk to her own when she hadn't thought very highly of him. Which all had to do with his Matusa demon heritage.

They were the highest order of demons, Kibiterons being beneath that, and Jared's Elantus demon beneath that. Then there was the ghostly Matusa that was hanging around close by. Even now, Hunter could vaguely see the demon in a shimmering ghostly aura, when before he couldn't.

Hunter knew it had to do with Alana's abilities somehow. The longer he was with her, the more he seemed to have more new abilities too.

As a ghost, Indigo walked through the leader of this rabble of so-called demon hunters.

"Hey, Mikey, they were talking about hunting demons. That's what we do, all right? Sheesh," one of the girls said.

Celeste, a Camaran demon, who could cloak her demon aura, and poison a Matusa's blood with her own, hadn't made it to the party tonight. They hadn't been able to get ahold of her, never saw her at school the rest of the day, and so they figured she had other business.

She would take off sometimes like that, and not tell the rest of them where she was going or what she was up to. She sometimes foretold future events, which would or wouldn't come in handy, depending on the trouble they found themselves in. But sometimes, she could change the future. Though they'd never seen any indication of that.

Alana was a witch and could deal with poltergeists, except for Indigo. If Hunter could have banished the annoying, full-blooded Matusa, he would have done so.

Samson, Samuria demon, insisted his job was to protect the Kubiteron gate guardian, which was Alana, but Hunter had assigned him the task of watching over Celeste. Not that Samson ever listened to him. In fact, there'd been a lot of insubordination when Hunter was the top demon kind and shouldn't tolerate any of it. He guessed it was his human half that was giving him all the trouble in allowing it.

"So, you know what we're looking for? Had any experience?" Mikey asked.

How could anyone take the kid seriously with a handle like that?

Hunter cast Alana a look.

"A little," Alana said. "Do you have a...summoning book or something?"

It was the demon hunters' mission to destroy summoning books whenever they heard of their existence. Then go after the summoner because some of them would memorize the summoning spell and wouldn't need the book any longer.

"You mean like Dean and Sam Winchester have?" Mikey asked.

"Who?" Alana arched a brow.

Whoever they were, if they had a summoning book, they needed to destroy it. The kid had lost Hunter too. He wondered just who these Winchester guys were and figured they would have to go after them next.

"You know, they go to the crossroads and bury a box, say a spell, and it summons a demon. Or they mark on a floor to capture the demon and do the same thing. They used to use a book, but they've captured so many of them, they've memorized the spells."

Which was always a real worry.

"Do you have a box like that?" Hunter asked, getting interested. But he also had to know more about these Winchesters.

"Yeah. But we haven't found the right crossroads, yet."

Alana glanced at Hunter. He shook his head. He hadn't ever heard of such a thing in all the time he'd been hunting for the summoners, freeing the demons who wanted to return to their world, and eliminating the volatile Matusa who wanted to stay and rule Earth world. But it didn't mean it didn't exist. They were always running into new troubles.

"Why would you want to summon a demon?" Alana asked, sounding both perplexed and irritated.

"Duh. We're demon hunters. We hunt demons. If we summon one, then we can make it tell us where the others are."

"In the demon world," Alana said. "Not here. Not unless they happen to run across one another. Bringing them here is crazy."

She was right. The summoners usually brought them here, thinking they could use them to do their bidding. And they could —unless they accidentally brought over a Matusa. They wouldn't be enslaved by anyone. And the summoner who thought so would learn quickly how fatal their mistake was.

"Haven't you ever watched *Supernatural*? Don't you know anything? The demons all group together and work as a team. Their eyes turn completely black, and the whites of the eyes disappear and—"

"What?" Alana frowned.

"Okay, look, if you don't watch *Supernatural,* which is your way to learn how it's done, then you're not demon hunters. Watch the show. Learn something. Then come back, and we'll give you the initiation. If you pass that, then you can join the team. But you'll have to be tested for six months before you're officially in," Mikey said.

Alana shook her head. "You've got to be kidding."

"What's the initiation?" Hunter had to ask.

Alana glanced back at Hunter's pickup and looked like she was ready to leave, figuring the kids would never get anywhere with really summoning a demon if they were basing it on some TV series.

But Hunter worried they would take this too far, find some innocent bystander and hurt the person, who was not a demon. Or even one of their own teammates accidentally.

"We have to make sure any new initiates aren't demons," Mikey said, his mouth curved in a small smile, almost demon acceptable.

Alana rolled her eyes.

Even though Hunter didn't think these kids could do anything to prove that he and his friends who made up the demon guardian team were demons or part demons, he still didn't like the idea. Though he did worry that if any of his team members got angry enough, their eyes would glow red. Apparently, that didn't prove anyone was a demon, not according to the television show.

Still, he could envision this bunch of kids quickly reevaluating their demon kind.

A girl tossed water on Alana.

"Hey, what's the big idea?" Alana shouted, and Hunter quickly took hold of her arm in a persuasive, "keep control of your demon temper" way. She turned her glowing red eyes on him, total turn on for him, and he smiled right back at her.

She quickly tamped down her anger, evidently seeing the red of her eyes reflecting off his.

"It's holy water. If you screamed out and burned up, we would know you were a demon," the girl said, brows arched.

Alana looked at the heavens above as if she wished to be taken away from all this idiocy.

"Hey, take this seriously or you're not in," Mikey said.

The girl threw something white at Alana, and she frowned as the white stuff stuck to her wet clothes.

"Salt. You would have burned up with that too. And the last test?" The girl pointed at the ground. "That's the symbol that the Winchesters always use to ensure a demon is captured. Then they can get the truth out of them. If you were a demon, you wouldn't be able to leave." She smiled.

Hunter didn't think the demon circle would hold them, but what if it did? "So you've never actually summoned a demon, caught one, or destroyed one?" Hunter asked.

"Oh, we've done the first two," Mikey said. "We just haven't destroyed it yet."

"You don't mean us, do you?" Alana wiped the salt off her arms, trying to sound amused, but Hunter swore she was having difficulty controlling her demon heritage. The way she was clenching her teeth and the way she smiled at them was not in the least bit reassuring. Then again, it could be her witch's heritage. He never could tell which one was more dangerous.

"No. Not you. We thought maybe the two of you were also. And that guy, Jared, and maybe even Samson," Mikey said, looking each of them over.

"What makes you think Jared or Samson is one? They're both just like the rest of us." But Hunter was getting bad vibes about this. They said they'd summoned a demon and captured it. Did they mean Celeste?

"Because *I'm* a master demon hunter, and I know these things. We're still not even sure about all of you," Mikey said. "You will have to be tested to make sure you're not one of them. But only after you learn how it's done. Watch the show and then return in three days."

"We'll be back," Hunter said, almost thinking of dropping the whole lot of them in the demon world so they could figure that out, and at least they couldn't hurt anyone here. What bothered him though, was that they thought they'd already caught a demon, and since they thought it was a friend of theirs, they had to find Celeste, or whoever the person was, if that was the case, and free him or her.

They headed to the vehicle, and Alana said to Hunter, "We have to find whoever they've captured if they're not lying about it. Where do we look first?"

"We need to find Celeste. I'm starting to worry about her," Hunter said. "If they believe she's a demon, and they've taken her prisoner, we've got to free her and deal with these nutcases."

"If it hadn't been for these guys, I might have figured she was off doing her own thing again. These guys could be a real danger to anyone they thought were demons, when they're just ordinary humans, Alana said."

They piled into the vehicle and drove off. "Do you see any sign of a Camaran's demon signature?" Hunter asked.

Alana glanced at her demon tracker. "Nope. Nothing. How will we find her or whoever they took hostage?"

"First, we look at the paper," Jared said.

"The paper?" Alana asked.

"For missing persons. The online newspaper."

"Or we could check at the police station." Alana kept watching her tracker to see if any demon signature showed up.

"Or I could hack into the police station computers." Jared smiled and began tapping away at his keyboard.

Everyone shook their heads. Hunter was always awed at all that Jared could do with computers. Though Jared felt the same about Hunter and the way he handled the Matusa demons.

"Okay..." Jared paused. "No one is missing. At least no one has been *reported* missing."

"So, either these kids lied, or they took a homeless person hostage? Or someone else like that who nobody would miss?" Alana asked.

"Celeste is missing," Hunter reminded them.

"She does this. Lots," Alana reminded him. "And no one would report her missing."

"Do you think they would be able to summon a demon?" Samson asked.

"No. If they had opened a portal to the demon world, it would have called me to it," Alana said.

Jared began playing something on his laptop. "Okay, the Winchesters don't know how to open a portal to summon demons. It's just a TV series."

"Good, so that means it's a false alarm," Samson said.

"Not if they're taking this seriously, and Mikey has taken Celeste, or someone else hostage," Hunter said. "When was the last time any of us saw her?"

Everyone looked at Alana because Celeste was now living with her and her mother. "This morning before I went to school. She made me eat breakfast with her. She didn't say anything about skipping school."

"Wouldn't she have had some vision of something bad happening?" Jared asked.

"No," Hunter said. "She told us she doesn't always have them. She might not have had one before she was taken. If she was taken."

"Okay, I'm going to try this and see if I can get ahold of her."

"Telepathically?" Hunter asked. It was a great gift Alana had, though he'd kind of felt special when he was the only one she could contact before.

"Yeah. She can't contact me back, but if she's close enough, I could tell her the problem we're facing, and we're worried she might be the one who's being held hostage. If she's not, she can tell us via a cell phone that she's not."

Everyone waited.

Alana shook her head. "I tried, and she's not 'picking up.' Unless she's lost her phone or is too far away to receive my message."

"Or is being held hostage," Hunter said, his voice dark.

4

With her hands tied behind her back around a wooden chair, her legs tied to the legs of the chair, and her mouth covered to keep her from screaming, Celeste considered the mess she was in. What good was being psychic if she couldn't see the visions earlier than they were occurring? Like literally minutes before the guy knocked her out, and she had no time to protect herself?

Yes, her type lived for danger—but that meant calculating the risks too. Didn't it?

Okay, so the fool vision told her that a bunch of loony teens from her school were attempting to torture another kid, who they thought was a demon. She had to save him. Just her. She knew so because she was the only one who was in her vision. Not her friends.

Why? Because she'd skipped classes again, the kid was near the park she was walking through, and she didn't have time to call on her friends to help her. It was a simple case of freeing the kid, and they would both take off. No one else was around the boy right now. It was just him, trapped in a basement. He appeared to be around sixteen, tied to a chair and gagged, terrified, his dark hair wet with perspiration, his brown eyes wild with fear.

She'd only had time to race into the house, find the stairs to the basement, and free him when they heard people's voices. She'd grabbed his hand and led him quietly up the stairs. Or at least tried to. Three of the steps creaked.

She hurried him the rest of the way up, and he dashed out the open front door before she could reach him. That's all she remembered. Except for something hitting her in the back of the head and making her black out.

She appeared to be in the basement of the same house. Concrete block walls surrounded her, one set of stairs, a single window high above, and no furniture, except the wooden chair she was tied to. There were no sounds up above, and whoever had taken her hostage had hit her in the head so hard, she'd been knocked out. She wasn't sure for how long, but her head still throbbed with renewed pain. She just hoped the boy had gotten away.

She wished she could reach her cell phone, still in her jacket pocket, but her hands were tied behind her back and no matter how much she tried to wriggle free, she couldn't. She wished she had some offensive abilities, more so than if her blood mixed with the blood of a Matusa's open wound, his would be poisoned and wouldn't coagulate, so it would run freely until he died. But that wouldn't do her any good with someone human. She wished she could telepathically communicate with Alana like Alana was now doing with her.

Celeste could cloak her demon type and pretend to be human, but that only worked with demons. Humans only believed she was human. Well, normally. This group of teens thought she was a demon. How had they come to that conclusion?

Unless she'd said something to one of her demon guardian team while at school about visiting the demon world to find her parents. She'd been so excited about it, she might have said something to Alana and hadn't guarded her speech like she should have.

Her chair was sitting in the middle of a circle, with salt placed around the outer edge. She guessed it meant she couldn't break free from the demon barrier they'd erected. Little did they know that nothing like that would stop her. Not like just plain old tying her hands behind her back had.

Man, she wished she could reach her phone, or turn into mist like Samson could, or become invisible, though when Jared did that, he was still his full solid self, so if she could do it, she would just be invisible and tied to a chair.

She wished she could destroy the chair or her ropes like Hunter and probably Alana could. Or be able to compel someone to do something like Alana could. She wished the ghostly Matusa could find her and report back to Alana, who could see and understand him, and tell her where Celeste was being held hostage.

She wished she could do anything that would get her out of the mess she was in.

"I swear, Mikey, they could be a help to us," she heard a girl finally say upstairs, as a door opened and shut and several footsteps followed on the wood floor above her.

"They're friends of a demon," Mikey said. "And you heard them talking about demon stuff. If they're friends of them, they're not going to hunt them down. That other kid she freed, couldn't have been one. He got outside the circle, and he didn't just vanish."

His voice...where had she heard Mikey's voice before? The name didn't register, but the voice sounded familiar.

"I still don't know how you know she's one. We tried all the usual stuff to check her out," a girl said. "And on that Alana friend of hers too."

"Yeah, and you heard Celeste. She was going to the demon world for spring break. She's a demon! She was telling Alana. So, she has got to be one too."

"Or Alana's under Celeste's control and just human. Once we kill the demon, Alana won't be under the demon's control any longer," the girl said.

"Get real, Anna. Once someone's controlled by a demon, she or he is always controlled by one."

Celeste wracked her brain to recall where she'd heard the voice before. Mikey. No Mikey. No...no...Bengal. Bengal? His voice was deeper now, but if it was him, he was an Elantus demon, her boyfriend when she was thirteen before she was moved again to a new foster home, a new city.

"If none of the stuff works to prove they're demons though, we can't be sure. We can't kill one just because we think one is. If we kill a human, we'll be in trouble."

Yes! But Celeste wasn't willing to be the guinea pig so they could learn what would prove she was a demon, or not if Mikey wasn't Bengal and she was just confused in thinking he was. Her head was still splitting in two, and she had to be mistaken.

If she could move beyond the circle, maybe they would realize she couldn't just disappear, and she couldn't be one. They hadn't even given her a chance to come up with a good story to explain the demon business she'd been discussing with Alana.

She rocked the chair until she was able to plant her feet on the cement floor. Then she tried hopping until she reached the edge of the circle, and fell outside of it, hoping to break the chair, but it was too sturdy. At least she was outside of the circle. That would prove she wasn't a demon, wouldn't it?

But if it was Bengal, he knew very well what she was.

She'd made such a racket, that the door to the basement creaked open.

Her heart was pounding like she'd run ten miles in a marathon. Surely, Alana and the rest of her friends would know she'd disappeared by now and was in trouble. She guessed she needed to let them know she would be gone and for what reason, now that she was part of the team. She'd been alone for so long, dealing with all these issues, that she wasn't used to sharing with others.

"She's outside of the circle!" Anna said.

They didn't come down the stairs like she'd anticipated, maybe afraid that once she was outside the circle, she could do terrible things to them. Like she could do anything to anyone while tied to a chair, her mouth still gagged? Get real.

She just hoped if they didn't aggravate her any more than she was already pissed off that her eyes would start glowing red.

"What do we do now?" Anna asked Mikey.

Run for your lives, Celeste wanted desperately to tell them.

"We can't reach her now, or she could eliminate us."

Good, so go!

She smelled smoke and heard the crackling of flames. She tried to wrench her wrists free from their confinement, but she couldn't. She kept trying, knowing that even if she hurt her wrists, she would heal quicker than humans, but she couldn't get loose. Were the ropes loosening a bit? Or was it her imagination? Mikey was a dead human, or demon if he really was Bengal.

She vowed never to go off on her own again, without informing her friends! If she survived the fire...which she realized she was envisioning...and it wasn't happening just yet. No smoke. No crackling.

"Okay, we've tried all the places we know of that Celeste goes to when she skips school and has to get away from it all." Alana didn't know how Celeste could manage to have future visions daily and live with them.

But she knew that sometimes Celeste had to get away to some-place quiet. At least that's what she told Alana. If Celeste's demon type sought danger, that didn't fit. Unless she had to get away to somewhere quiet to figure out what her psychic visions meant and what she could do to change the future.

Was that what had happened? She'd seen something and had run headlong into danger?

Without telling them?

"They have to have taken Celeste," Alana said. "Okay, we have to learn what Mikey's last name is and where he lives. Who his friends are. If we go after his friends, they would probably be more likely to fold under pressure than he would."

"Then that's our next mission," Hunter said.

Jared was on it. He passed out the addresses to everyone.

"Everyone pair up. Alana's with me," Hunter said.

"I'm Alana's—"

"Don't say it, Samson. You're with Jared." Hunter looked at the list. "We're going to take this half of the list. Send it to me, Jared."

"That includes Mikey."

"Right. We'll go after a couple of others first. Anna, first, and then go from there," Hunter said. "Let's go."

"Anna's one of the girls who solicited us to join the group. We sat with her at lunch," Alana said, going to Hunter's black pickup.

Jared and Samson went in his neon yellow Jeep, but Jared didn't look happy about going with him. He and Hunter had worked so long together that he didn't like that Hunter wanted to do as much as he did with Alana.

Alana wished Jared or Samson would get interested in Celeste the way that Hunter was interested in her, but Celeste had to be around more too. She thought Celeste still didn't feel part of the group yet.

"Do you think Jared is all right?" she asked Hunter.

He gave her a dark look. "About what? We have a mission to complete, and he knows it."

"Yeah, but he has worked with you for years."

"He'll have to get used to it. We work together, sometimes separately, sometimes with other teammates, whatever the situation calls for."

"All right. I'm just saying that sometimes I think his feelings get hurt."

"He's a full demon."

"He's not a Matusa. But even *they* have feelings."

Hunter snorted. "Are you still trying to reach Celeste telepathically?"

"Yes. And I keep calling her cell." Alana was looking at the demon tracker also. "She has to be some distance away as we can't... wait, I'm seeing a signature! It's a Camaran's signature!"

"And there's an old house on fire straight ahead."

"That's...that's where she is! It's got to be her." Alana's heart was drumming in her ears, and she quickly contacted Samson. "I found her. I believe. But a house is burning, and I think she's at the same location."

"I was using Jared's tracker, and we finally saw her signature, and yours too. We're not too far behind you."

As soon as Hunter slammed on his brakes in front of the abandoned house, Alana jumped out of the vehicle.

"Wait, Alana!" Hunter wished he had more control over her.

She immediately began using a water spell to douse the burning house.

"These people are vicious," Hunter said.

"If we can get their ringleader, that might be the end of it."

Jared slammed on his brakes, his Jeep skidding to a halt. Both he and Samson jumped out of the Jeep. Hunter raced toward the burning house.

"Hunter!" Alana shouted.

Now she had to know how he felt when she did crazy stuff that put her life in danger.

She doused him with water, and he ran into the burning house.

"Celeste!" he yelled out, but she didn't answer. He pulled out his tracker and, in the smoke, the light of the tracker helped him to see she was down in a basement. "I'm coming!" The place was filled with smoke, and he raced down the stairs, barely able to see. Staying low, he saw a window. As soon as he saw it, the glass shattered.

Jared hollered from the broken window, "Are you in the basement, Hunter? That's where she is."

"Yeah." Then Hunter saw her tied to a chair. She'd better not be dead. "Celeste! I found her!" He cut the ropes binding her and pulled off her gag. "Celeste."

Her eyelids fluttered, but she didn't open them. Her heartbeat was faint. He needed to get her out of the burning house. Some of the roof collapsed, and they heard sirens. He needed to get her out of there before anyone discovered they were there. After all the business last time with Alana being found in the vicinity of a murdered man at the zoo, they didn't need to be found at the site of a burning house.

"We've got company," Jared hollered.

As if Hunter didn't know it already.

Mist sifted in through the house and suddenly Samson was there. "Let me help you."

Hunter had Celeste in his arms, and he didn't need Samson's help at this point. Unless he knew CPR.

"I'm good."

The house was in flames, but Alana was concentrating on casting water on the part of the house where he and Samson were so that when they ran outside with Celeste, they were dripping with water and black soot.

"Get her in your pickup, and I'll do what I can," Alana said, hurrying to jump in the back seat of his pickup.

He laid Celeste back there with her, and Alana began to give her CPR.

Hunter jumped into the driver's seat. "Go, go, go!" he shouted to Jared and Samson, both of whom were running for Jared's Jeep.

The two vehicles tore off away from the house, and he hoped no one caught sight of their license plates before they disappeared down the road. Jared's Jeep was way too conspicuous.

"How is she?" Hunter prayed they had reached her in time.

Celeste began to cough.

"She's going to be fine, but we need to take her home, now."

"Not to an emergency room?"

"No. We'll take care of her. She has suffered from smoke inhalation, but we can't take her to a hospital, or they'll know that she's been in a burning house. Recently."

"Can you take care of her?"

"I'm a healer, remember?"

Celeste looked pasty gray. He hoped Alana knew what she was doing. So far, they hadn't lost one of their teammates. They'd been lucky. He didn't want to lose any of them now. Since he was in charge of them, he was the one who was ultimately responsible.

Alana reached over the seat and rubbed Hunter's shoulder. "We'll get the people who did this."

"Yeah, we will." Hunter had every intention of going after them. Now.

Alana shook her head. "Listen, I know you well enough that I'm sure you plan to tear after them on your own. You can't. Look at what happened to Celeste when she was by herself. Yeah, yeah, before you say anything, I know that you believe she's just a Camaran and you're a deadly Matusa, so she didn't stand a chance, but you do."

Hunter let out his breath.

"We need to learn who did this to her before you take off after them. And you need to take Jared and Samson with you. I'll call my mom, and she can help protect us if you're worried anyone might come after us," Alana said.

"Yeah, I am, and Samson is supposed to guard you." Hunter didn't like it, but he could run into more trouble than he bargained for if he went off on his own. Alana was right that they needed to know who had done this to Celeste.

Celeste coughed again.

"I would rather you take both of them with you." Their breaths frosted and she said, "Indigo's with us."

He was useless most of the time, but Hunter didn't voice his opinion this time out loud. For once, he wished the ghostly Matusa could help them, but he knew he would still have wanted Alana for his own.

He parked at Alana's home and hurried to carry Celeste into the house. Alana was already rushing to the door to unlock it, and she was on the phone with her mother. "Yes, yes, can you come home now? We might need some of your spells in case we have trouble. No, not against bad demons. Against bad humans. So, it shouldn't be that difficult a job. Celeste was hurt bad." She followed Hunter into the house, and he hesitated, not knowing where to carry Celeste.

"Her room—"

"Living room," Celeste choked out. "I don't...want...to be... alone."

"Let me get a blanket to wrap her in," Alana said.

He figured Alana didn't want Celeste to make a mess of the couch, her clothes no longer dripping water, but she was damp and sooty.

Jared and Samson barged into the place. "How is she?" both asked at the same time.

"I'll live." Celeste's voice was raspy and barely audible. She coughed some more.

Alana spread a blanket on the couch, then wrapped Celeste's wet hair in a towel. She covered her with another blanket. "Who did this to you?"

"Mikey. Anna was with him. But she was against..." Celeste coughed. "Against hurting me. Unsure if I was a demon."

"They didn't see your red eyes?" Jared asked.

She shook her head. "Mikey's..." She coughed again, tears in her eyes. "He's an Elantus demon."

Everyone stared at her like she was nuts.

"He looked human when we saw him," Jared said. "Why would he try to kill you?"

"Ex-boyfriend. He can cloak his demon heritage so he looks like a human."

Hunter swore under his breath. "Okay, so he was hiding his demon aura when we met him. Like you can do."

"Yes."

"Has he always lived here?" Hunter asked.

"Years. I met him...when I was thirteen. He's not...like me, exactly. Not like...Jared. Why would he hurt...a human? Unless the teen somehow...knew he was a demon?"

Hunter rubbed his chin in thought. "Because the kid angered him, maybe? Why would Mikey start up a demon hunter group?"

"It amused him?" Celeste coughed, then closed her eyes. "He has a dark sense of humor. Darker than most of us."

"Do you know where they are?"

"He...he set fire to the place. I...freed a teen they had tortured."

Hunter crouched before her, frowning. "Who was the teen?"

Celeste opened her brown eyes, filled with tears. "Someone... wearing one of our...school T-shirts, but he appeared...younger than us."

Hunter ran his hands through his hair. "Okay, so the teen got away. Who's to say they won't grab him again and try to kill him? This has to stop."

"What do you plan to do?" Alana asked.

"He wants to find demons and question them? If he pretends to be a demon hunter when he knows just who is a demon already because he's already one, I'll allow him to identify all the demons he wants," Hunter said.

"You're going to send him back to the demon world," Alana said.

"Yeah. Perfect justice. He doesn't belong here. He'll go back. He's a full demon, right, Celeste?"

"Yes. As far as I know."

"And the others?" Alana asked.

"We'll see if they continue to pursue this business with the demons. If they lose their leader and don't go any further with this, then we can let it go. But if they continue demon hunting, we'll have to take care of the new leader or leaders," Hunter said.

"Sounds like a plan to me," Jared said.

"I should stay here with Alana and Celeste," Samson said.

"No. You go with Hunter and Jared. My mother will be arriving soon. We'll be fine. Go. Get him. Before he can hurt anyone else."

"Maybe you should clean up a bit, Hunter," Jared said. "Or the Elantus demon might figure we were at the burning house. Keep him guessing. If he is a demon, we don't want him to know that we know. If he thinks you might have saved Celeste, and she might have figured out who he was, we wouldn't have the advantage."

"Feel free to use the guest bathroom, Hunter. I'm going to help Celeste wash up once she feels better," Alana said.

Hunter walked into the bathroom, shut the door, and looked in the mirror. He couldn't believe what a mess he was. He looked like he'd been in a firefight and barely made it out alive. He stripped off his clothes and took a shower.

When he came out of the shower, his clothes were gone.

"Where are my clothes!" If Alana thought to steal his clothes so he wouldn't go after Mikey, she was mistaken. He wrapped a towel around his waist and opened the door.

Jared headed into the house with a change of clothes for Hunter. "That's the bag you always keep in your truck."

"Thanks." Hunter took the bag and closed the bathroom door. He'd learned long ago to always carry extra clothes in the line of work he did. Though being covered in soot was something he'd never considered. But he'd fought with a Matusa who had poisoned him once and his claws had torn up his shirt, and he'd bled all over it. So a change of clothes had been essential for difficult jobs.

After dressing, he came out of the bathroom and was glad to see Alana's mother had arrived home. She was fussing over Celeste who was cleaned up now and wearing fresh clothes.

"Alana told me what happened. Go get him," her mother said.

"We're on it." Hunter pulled Alana into a hug and kissed her. "Stay safe."

"I will, Hunter. You too." She kissed him back.

He released her and headed back outside to his pickup, torn about leaving her behind in case she was pulled to a portal and taking her with him and putting her in danger.

"Two vehicles?" Jared asked.

"Yeah, a show of force and to track him better if he runs. We'll use his parents' address to see if he's there," Hunter said.

They drove off, headed for Mikey's house, ready to show him what a Matusa demon could really do.

lana worried about Hunter, just as much as she knew he always worried about her when they had to deal with something like this. Well, maybe not exactly something like this. It was a shame that Mikey's parents would lose a son, but if he was truly a demon and one with evil intentions, they were better off without him.

"So, the teen you rescued wasn't a demon?" Alana asked Celeste, who was drying out her long hair.

"No. He was just an ordinary teen. Unless he can cloak his aura also. I didn't have time to ask him why they thought he was a demon when I freed him. He escaped, and they took me down too fast after that," Celeste said.

"What if he lured you there?"

"I had a future vision."

"Oh. And you tried to change the future?"

"I saw the burning house, the teen. Oftentimes my visions are confusing. Disjointed. I thought the teen was going to die in the burning house. After I rescued him, I wondered if I was the one who was going to die in the burning house, not the boy. Did I change the future by freeing him? I don't know."

"Hmm, sounds like you might have."

Alana's mom was erecting barrier spells so that they would be warned if anyone tried to breach the place without an invitation. She had the barrier spells fine-tuned so that certain people would be able to enter at will—Alana's friends, for instance.

Alana had used her healing abilities on Celeste's throat and lungs, ridding her of the smoke that had filled them earlier. Celeste was still coughing some though. Alana had helped heal the trauma to the back of Celeste's head also.

"Would you girls like something to drink?" Alana's mom asked.

"Lemon and ginger tea," Alana said. "With honey for Celeste."

Celeste shook her head. "I don't—"

"Medicinal tea," Alana told Celeste. "It will help soothe your irritated throat and take away the taste of smoke in your mouth. I can't believe one of our schoolmates would do something like this. I mean, if he has lived among us for a long time, why suddenly attack humans or his own kind?"

"I don't know. I've been trying to figure it out since I freed the teen. I thought I saw Mikey at school, only he wasn't called that when I'd met him. His name is Bengal. At least, it was. Maybe that was a made-up name too. We'd been friends in school, a different school, another city. When I had to move to another city halfway across the States, I didn't see him again. We were thirteen at the time. Now I'm here, and I couldn't believe he could be also. I tried following him, but I lost him in the crowd."

"Why didn't you tell us?"

"What? That an old boyfriend had just shown up?"

"He's a demon," Alana said. "We need to keep track of them. He has to be cloaking his demon aura like you can do. Why would he, I wonder? Only demons would be able to see him. If he has nothing to hide from us, why would he conceal his aura?"

"I did it when I was around you and your friends. I didn't know how you would treat me."

"Why hunt our kind of demons? If that's what he's doing. And he must know that based on our demon types. Well, except for Hunter. We don't harm anyone."

"I don't know. Unless Hunter is the reason for Mikey concealing his demon aura. Most lesser demons, not that I think of myself that way—though when I couldn't save myself, I did feel somewhat impotent. But most would fear him for being one of the Dark Ones."

"Then why confront Hunter? Mikey had to know what he was and how dangerous that could be. It doesn't make any sense. Unless..."

"Unless what?"

"Unless he's cloaking his demon kind with another."

"A Matusa?" Celeste sounded like she couldn't believe it.

"Yeah. One cloaked himself so I thought he was a Kubiteron, like my father. He pretended to be my father. But he was a Matusa."

Alana's mother served them tea and cookies. "You're not still going to Seplichus for spring break now, are you?"

"Yeah, we are. We don't know if we'll find anyone we're looking for, but we have to try." Alana knew her mother was more than concerned about losing her. But she couldn't live her life as if at any moment she would be torn away from the ones she loved. She'd be a basket case. And Alana needed her father to help her control when she was pulled to portals.

"With all those Matusa after you?" her mother asked.

"We're going to portal jump around. Jared's been to the Hall of Records the most. Samson is from Seplichus..."

"Not from that part of the world, from what I understand," her mom reminded her.

"No, from a village that bordered a swamp. But he knows how to deal with demons since he'd lived there all his life before he showed up in our lives."

"That's only a few days from now. Celeste, do you think you can still go?" Alana's mom asked.

"Sure. More than ever. It reminds me how scary Earth world can be. Forget about how scary Seplichus can be. I didn't think I wanted to see my parents because I didn't want to move back to the demon world if I found them. Wouldn't they be heartbroken if I found them and left them behind? Wouldn't I be also? I've lived here since I was three years old, and I don't know anything about my world," Celeste said.

"True, but if I'd lost my daughter all those years ago, I would still be grieving, wishing I could see her and make a connection. Hunter can always open a portal and take you back there to see your family if you prefer living here."

"And I can," Alana said.

"You have trouble every time you go there," her mother said.

"I do, but if she needed me to, I could take her. Not that I have to, or that I'm going to, but I do have the ability."

"I know, but it would be better if Hunter took her."

"Hey," Celeste said, changing the subject. "do you want to watch *Supernatural* and see what the demon hunters think works against us?"

Alana switched on the TV. "Yeah, but I'm not joining *their* demon-hunting team."

Hunter hoped that taking out the head honcho would mean the end of their little gang of demon hunters, but first, they had to locate Mikey. When they reached his red-brick, two-story home, Hunter knocked on the door.

A middle-aged gentleman opened the door. "Yes?"

"Is Mikey at home? He's our friend from high school." Hunter was glad he'd cleaned up and changed clothes. He could imagine what Mikey's father would think if he hadn't.

"No. He's staying at a friend's house for the night. Buzz Carpenter. He's five houses down to our left, this side of the street."

"Thanks," Hunter said, then they drove down to that house.

He knocked on the door there, but a woman said, "No, I haven't seen Mikey in a while. A week or two? He's not here."

Someone was lying. Now Hunter wished Alana was with him so she could compel Mikey's dad to tell them the truth. Then he smiled. He could bring her here. He opened a portal.

"What are you doing?" Jared asked, sounding shocked.

"Calling on—"

"What...?" Alana glowered at Hunter and jabbed her finger at his chest. "Don't you dare call me like this again."

"We're getting conflicting stories. She says she hasn't seen Mikey. His dad said he had been over here. Hurry, before anyone notices the portal."

She compelled the woman to speak the truth, but she said the same thing that Hunter had heard already. Then she made the woman forget everything she'd seen and heard.

Hunter closed the portal and grabbed Alana's arm as if to make her stay with him.

"First, you don't want me with you. *Then* you want me with you. Make up your mind." Alana glowered at Hunter, and he knew she didn't like it when he forced her to join him by opening a portal. He also knew she would get over it quickly enough if she could aid them in their mission. She didn't like being left behind.

"We don't want you with us," Jared supplied. "But sometimes you're a necessary evil."

Alana smiled at him. Then she scowled, got into the pickup, and Hunter drove her to the other house, Jared and Samson following in the Jeep. She wasn't usually able to do this either. If her astral self was to go anywhere, he would have to open another portal. It was scary to think things kept changing for her, and they never knew what to expect.

When they knocked at the door, this time, they got the mom, and she didn't look anything like Mikey. Nor did the dad, so Celeste could be right. These people weren't Mikey's real family.

"Tell us where Mikey is," Alana said.

"My husband told you that he—"

"*Tell* us where Mikey is," Alana repeated. "The truth."

"Mikey is at that old, abandoned house where he and his friends like to play."

"Thank you."

Which was no help at all since Mikey had burned down the place.

"Where else would he go?" Alana asked.

"Home? Anna's house, maybe. Another old, abandoned house."

"What's Anna's address? And where is the other old, abandoned house?" Alana asked.

The woman gave her the locations.

"Thank you. You will forget you have spoken to us, and that you have seen us. Go inside and do whatever you planned to do."

The woman closed the door.

"We will split forces. Alana and I will go to the abandoned house. Jared, you and Samson go to Anna's house. Learn from her if there's somewhere else he might go."

"Wait," Alana said. "I need to return to my body."

"Maybe it would be safer for you if you—"

She folded her arms, her eyes glowing red.

"You guys, go."

Jared saluted Hunter.

Samson said to Alana, "I could take you back to your body and Hunter could go with Jared."

Hunter gave him a look that said if he wanted to be on their team, and didn't want to see just how angry he could get—being that he was a Matusa—they did things his way.

"Just saying," Samson said, and climbed into the Jeep with Jared.

Before Hunter could drive Alana back to her home, she vanished.

"Alana!"

"Home. You'd better come and get me and not go to the other abandoned house by yourself."

To keep her from danger...it was tempting.

6

As soon as Hunter picked up Alana at her house, they headed to the next abandoned house.

"Thanks for picking me up to take me with you," Alana said, knowing what the Dark One was thinking. He should have left her home and done this by himself.

"Against my better judgment."

"You know, if you think I will be yours, you have to agree that we're a team."

He gave her a hint of a dark smile. "We are."

"Okay, so I was talking to Celeste about this, and I was wondering, what if this guy is a Matusa."

Hunter frowned at her.

"Yeah, I know, what are the odds? But remember the one who pretended—"

"To be your father. *Hell.* And the guy did act interested in you."

"Because I'm a Kubiteron. So, what if this guy hid his aura from us like Celeste did—and we thought he was human. But like the Matusa who pretended to be a Kubiteron, he could cloak his aura with another demon type when he saw her earlier. What if this guy can do both? A master at deception."

"He called himself a master demon hunter."

"But he isn't. I bet you anything he's an evil one."

"Why bother with the gathering of teens to hunt down demons and then eliminate them?"

"A sick joke? He's what? Eighteen or nineteen like you?"

"Yeah."

"He's young, trying to find his place in the world. He's a demon, laughing at the gullible teens he has recruited to get rid of his kind. If he truly is a Matusa, the only kind of demon I would think would go after humans like this, he's dangerous, especially if he isn't half-human like you. Though humans can be just as dangerous. Then he sees some of us and realizes there are other demons in the school. Now he's not so special. Not when you're just like him."

"I can't cloak my demon type, or make it appear to other demons that I'm human."

"Maybe you can, but you haven't learned how yet. Or maybe you're a slow learner when it comes to that."

He gave her a disgruntled look.

She smiled at him. Then she got serious. "Okay, so then what do we do? Send him to the demon world? He'll have to learn to make a way for himself in Seplichus?"

"Yeah. He won't find it easy, but he won't be hurting people here then. What about the teen that Celeste saved?"

"She said she didn't know why they thought he was a demon. Which means, she didn't see a demon aura."

"Okay, back it up to the business with Celeste."

"She dated Mikey when she was thirteen, and she thought he was an Elantus demon. But she had the vision of seeing the kid in trouble, so she went to rescue him."

"Still, that's a big coincidence, that she was 'called' upon to rescue the teen in the abandoned house, and then taken prisoner. And the guy who took her prisoner was her former boyfriend."

"Maybe he didn't know that her blood could poison his when

she's a Camaran. If he has lived here since he was little, he might not know everything about demon types, just like I was clueless."

"You didn't even know what you were."

"Exactly. Even Jared, who keeps a record of characteristics demon types supposedly have, didn't know that a Camaran demon's blood could poison a Matusa's. Which reminds me, if she gets cut, you don't get near her."

"You don't have to tell me twice."

But she knew Hunter. If Celeste was bleeding, Hunter would go to her aid. "It makes me wonder, again, if Jared's notion of fitting us into demon characteristic boxes is a mistake. That each of us is unique in our own way. Some might have a predisposition for certain traits, but it doesn't mean there isn't a crossover. What if you have some Elantus demon in your roots way back, for instance."

Hunter gave her a dark look.

She chuckled. He hated being one of the Matusa, yet he used it to his advantage also. The idea he had other kinds of demons in his bloodline—lesser demons—didn't seem to agree. "The house should be around the bend in this road, right past those woods," she said.

"Okay."

"Maybe you should let me out here, and I can sneak around the house."

"We stick together. I will park here, and we can walk over there together." Hunter stopped the truck on the side of the road. "Can you put a barrier around the truck?"

"I sure can." They left the truck, and she cast an invisible barrier around it to keep anyone from trying to steal it.

Red and gold leaves floated to the ground as they crunched on the already fallen leaves. Through the half-barren trees, they saw the abandoned house, two-story, wrap-around porch, the white siding turning to gray, lace curtains tattered, most of the windows broken, and the wooden steps splintered.

Near the side of the house, they saw two vehicles and heard movement in one of the rooms in the front of the house. They headed around the back of the house.

Inside, a girl was arguing with a guy. "*Anna and Mikey*," Alana said telepathically to Hunter, recognizing their voices.

"You didn't have to kill her," Anna said. If Mikey was a Matusa, she'd better watch what she said to him.

"She was a demon. That's our job."

"What if she wasn't? She got out of the circle!"

"Either you listen to me, or you're off the team."

"What of her friends? They'll be looking for her."

"All demons. We'll deal with them too."

"Really." Hunter pulled open the back door and walked into what was once a living room, the floors and walls bare. "I don't think so."

Alana was right beside him.

The girl dropped her can of soda on the floor and squeaked. The guy raised his hands to cast a spell, and Alana immediately opened the portal behind Mikey. Hunter rushed forth and using one of his ju-jitsu moves, slammed his boot into Mikey's stomach, propelling him into the demon world. Alana quickly closed the portal.

Hunter turned on Anna. "Are you a demon?"

She shook her head, staring at Hunter as if she were seeing a monster. Tears filled her eyes, and she shook uncontrollably. "What...what did you do to Mikey?"

"Sent him to the demon world, and you're next if you're a demon too."

She sat hard on her butt on the floor. "No! I'm not a demon. Sheesh. We're hunting them. He...he was a demon hunter. What have you done?" Anna's face was pasty white, her blue eyes huge.

They hadn't discussed what to do next, but Alana wanted to learn all she could from Anna before she decided to leave. If Mikey was a demon undercover, Anna could be also. She didn't appear to be though, as much as she seemed in shock and terrified.

"What we've done is saved you. If you know what's good for you, you'll disband this group, and forget you were ever involved in something so atrocious. You tortured a teen and killed another, burned her up in a fire. You'll have to live with that for the rest of your miserable life. *You're* pure evil," Hunter said.

"She...she was a demon. Mikey said so."

"You know that's not true," Alana said. "You know that Mikey was lying. In his demonic way, he was making you believe what he wanted you to."

She sobbed. "He...he tricked us? What...what are you?"

Hunter frowned at her. "Demon hunters. *Real* demon hunters who don't watch TV shows to learn the tricks of the trade. Mikey was the worst kind of demon. You're lucky to be alive. Now get out of here, tell the others Mikey was a demon and was sent back to his world. But know this, if someone manages to summon forth a demon, they'll pay with their lives. This isn't a game. And if Mikey can come through another portal..." Hunter shook his head. "Just hope that he doesn't."

Anna slowly nodded.

"I don't know. Maybe we're making a deadly mistake by allowing her to walk. Maybe we should send *her* to the demon world." Alana glanced at Hunter. "After what she did to our friend, our demon hunter friend, Anna's no better than the evil demons we've had to deal with."

Hunter stared the girl down.

Alana didn't mean it. She was all for giving the human girl another chance because she had tried to stop Mikey from killing Celeste. But Alana wanted to impress upon her how Anna had been brainwashed so easily and followed the Matusa, helping him with his evil plans. He hadn't compelled her to believe anything. She'd done it of her own free will, and even now, she was defending him. But she would never survive long in the demon world.

"No...no, I'll tell the others that we were taken in by a demon." Anna looked stricken, glancing at Hunter as if she thought he would save her from Alana when Hunter was much more of a threat to her. Usually.

"Really, can we afford to let her and the others loose on the world? What if she thinks she can take Mikey's place? What if she's stupid enough to believe Mikey again if he manages to return?" Alana asked Hunter as if Anna wasn't even there.

"I...I won't. He...he can't, can he?" Anna asked, sounding worried that if she betrayed him, he would come back and kill her.

"You'd better pray he doesn't," Hunter said. "We'll give you this one last chance. If we learn that you are attempting to summon demons or take anyone else hostage, believing them to be demons, all of you will be sent to the demon world. Believe me, you wouldn't last a second in their world."

"No...no, okay. All right. Just...let me go. Please. Please. I won't do any of this again. I promise."

"Who was the boy that you were torturing in the basement?" Alana asked.

"A demon. And your friend Celeste let him go."

"If he had been a demon, he would have destroyed you once he was beyond the circle of salt. He was no more a demon than you or me," Alana lied. "Why did Mikey say he was a demon?"

"His eyes turned all black."

"Well, they didn't. How hard was it to kidnap him?"

"We...we didn't have any trouble kidnapping him."

"Do you think a real demon would have allowed it?" Alana asked.

Anna shook her head.

"Exactly. Mikey was lying. What was the boy's name?" Alana loved it when Hunter let her be in charge. She was angry enough that Mikey had tried to kill Celeste that she was trying to tamp down the glowing red eyes bit.

"Wendell Compton. He's...in the gifted classes. He's supposed to be a sophomore, but he's in the senior classes."

"Did Mikey have a grudge against him?" Alana figured that had to be the reason.

"Uh, yeah. Wendell told him that he was a fake. That he was conning us all into believing he was a demon hunter."

"And you believed Mikey before you believed a smart guy?" Alana said it in a way that told the girl that she thought she was an idiot. She moved closer to the girl, and Anna quickly stood. "You saw Mikey for what he is. A monster. Hideous. A demon that you can recognize. Remember what I say."

"I remember."

"As to us, you saw nothing. When you see us in school, you don't remember anything about our business here. Mikey disappeared through the lights of a portal before escaping back to the demon world. You never saw us here."

Anna nodded.

"You will leave now and when you reach home, you'll text your friends and tell them that Mikey was a demon, that he opened a hole into his world and escaped back to it, that he nearly killed Celeste, except you saved her after she saved Wendell. That Wendell isn't a demon, just a smart kid that Mikey had a grudge against. That you no longer can hunt demons, or you'll die. Go now."

Anna scrambled out of the abandoned house, got in her car, and drove off.

"You let her off the hook on that one." Hunter sounded as though he wasn't certain that was a good idea.

"I didn't want to have to deal with all the craziness at school whenever they look at us and think we are demon hunters. Real ones. Some might want to even make amends and join us in the fight against the Matusa. What a mess that would be. Hopefully, Mikey won't return, and they will find something worthwhile to do with their lives. What do we do about Mikey's truck?" Alana asked.

"Leave it. His parents or the police will find it eventually." Hunter texted someone. "Okay, I let Jared know we're done with this." He got a text back and smiled.

"What?" Alana climbed into Hunter's truck.

Hunter texted Jared back. "He asked if you were up to your witchy stuff again. He wants to know all the details. I told him we would meet at your house and discuss what happened. We have three more days of school before we leave on spring break. Do you think we can manage that?"

"If no one opens any more portals while I'm in class, sure."

"We'll have to see if the 'demon hunters' at school are still making any plans."

"And see what happens between Wendell and Celeste. Hopefully, nothing, but if we have too much trouble with him, Anna, and the rest of her cohorts, I'll have to make them forget everything. That means we'll have to learn who all was in their group. Hopefully, it won't come to that," Alana said.

She hoped it wouldn't be because she had to change each of the faux demon hunters' minds, that could be a real challenge without anyone else being aware of what she was doing. She couldn't use her witch's skills to compel a mass group of people to do something. Not yet.

That was one nice thing about going to a human school. No one knew she was a witch. Half witch.

amson was given the task of following Celeste all around at school the next morning when she wanted to skip classes. After what had happened with trying to save Wendell, and nearly dying of smoke inhalation, and the concern that Anna or her friends would still think she was a demon, just like they thought Wendell was, she didn't want to go to school.

Celeste still couldn't wrap her mind around Alana's ability that she could wipe people's minds of what they'd seen or heard.

The first person she saw that morning was Anna. The girl looked stricken to see her and immediately, she and two of her buds headed in another direction. Then Celeste saw Wendell. He was watching her, looking like he wanted to approach her, but not.

"Coward," Samson said under his breath.

"He probably doesn't trust anyone at the school after what happened to him. Unless you mean *me*, and you'd *better* not," Celeste said.

Samson cast Celeste a small smile, then narrowed his eyes as he observed the teen. "I thought you said he'd been tortured. He looks perfectly healthy to me."

Celeste agreed. He'd had a gash across his forehead, burn

marks on his neck, and the same on his hands. Even from this distance, he looked like he didn't have any injuries. "Wait here for me."

"Hunter told me to stick to you like chewing gum."

"Do you always do what Hunter wants?" She knew Samson didn't.

"When it suits me. I'm to protect you. It's what Alana wants."

"You want it. But I'm afraid you'll scare him off. Stay here. I'll speak with him. Alone."

"All right, but if he's a demon..."

"If he is, he couldn't protect himself against Mikey." Celeste stalked across the hall, ignoring anyone in her path. With annoyed looks and caustic comments, most of the students moved out of her way.

She bumped into a girl who was one of the "demon hunters," and when the girl acted like she was going to shove her back for the insult, Celeste turned on her and said, "If you want to go to prison for torturing Wendell, and being part of a gang that tried to burn me up in that old abandoned house, go for it. I'll testify against you and every one of your little band of terrorists. You belong in jail. For life."

A group of kids heard Celeste telling the girl that, and her face turned red. She quickly departed the area. Celeste was afraid Wendell would have left the area, fearful of being seen with her, but he was just waiting in the same spot, not approaching her, just watching her.

"I'm glad you're okay," Celeste said. "I'm—"

"A Camaran." Wendell snorted. "My worst nightmare has been realized."

She frowned at him. "I saved your life."

"I hoped I could avoid being around any of you, and just live my life like any other normal kid."

"You're one of us? But I can't see your"—Celeste glanced

around—"type." Then she saw he was a Camaran like her. She smiled, then frowned. "Why didn't you come and talk to me, to any of us?"

"Are you kidding? A Matusa is in charge of you."

She snorted. "He's a friend. Hell, when I was dying in that abandoned house, Hunter was the one who saved me. Not you."

"He's *still* a Matusa."

"Half. He's half-human. How did you get here? *When* did you get here?"

"Last year. I got pulled in through a portal. I don't have any way back, and the summoner got so scared that the summoning worked, she shut the portal before any more of us came through, dropped her book, and fled. I tried using the summoning book to open the portal, but I couldn't get it to work. Anna told me how sorry she was for what they'd done to me and told me Mikey was a demon. He opened a door to the demon world and disappeared. I don't know how he did it."

"Alana sent him back. Mikey couldn't have done it, nor would he want to."

"The Kubiteron? She can open a portal?"

"Yes. Hunter can too. Both are half human."

"So, Mikey was a demon?"

"He *is* and he was hiding his aura like you were doing. I dated the creep when I was thirteen. He appeared to be an Elantus like Jared. At least that's what I thought. Some demons can camouflage their demon types with something else that makes them seem...less dangerous."

Wendell's blue eyes widened. "Not a Matusa."

"Like a Matusa, yes. Who else would want to hide their demon type when they are around other demons?"

Wendell still looked a little shaken by the news. "How did you know where I would be? Did you follow Mikey?"

"No. I had a future vision and saw you in trouble. I had to learn where you were. I only see bits and pieces, or I would have shown up sooner. Mikey didn't like that I'd messed up his plans."

"Future vision. Wow. I put him down in front of the others. I had no idea he was a demon. A Matusa."

"Maybe. He never acted like he was interested in Alana, did he? You know, all demon types are supposed to be drawn to her."

"I don't think he'd seen her at school. I'm sure he would have made a play for it if he had, even though Hunter is a Matusa. Can they get me back to my world?" Wendell asked.

"We can ask. That's what they do. They help lesser demons—not that I think any of us are—to return to the demon world and force the Matusa back there if they manage to get here. Sometimes they have to end their miserable lives."

"What about you?"

The bell rang, and Celeste ignored it. "I do anything I can to help them. I've only been with them for a short time. They've made me feel welcome, but I've been on my own, in other words, not been with our kind in so long, that I still need to get off alone. Some of it is because of the visions I have too, though."

"I want to meet Alana and see if she can send me back."

"Alana? Figures."

"Not because she's a Kubiteron. But because she can send me home."

"And you're afraid of Hunter. He's dangerous, but not to any of us who are here to help our kind and the humans."

"Classes," a teacher said to Celeste and Wendell.

"Yes, ma'am," Wendell said, then he began to walk backward toward a class.

She went after him, and he frowned at her.

Samson headed for them.

She took Wendell's hand. "I figure you're too young for me, but what the heck."

"How old do you think I am?" Wendell asked, frowning at her as she walked him to class.

"Sixteen?"

He snorted. "Twenty-one. I just look young. It drives me crazy. Everyone thinks I'm so young and without an ID to prove how old I am, they stuck me in school with sixteen-year-olds. I proved I knew too much, and they moved me to the senior class. How old are you?"

"Same age. I've moved around so much with foster families, that I'm behind."

"And you skip classes all the time."

"Future visions. They hit me at any time. It makes it difficult to concentrate on classes when I'm zoned out in another world."

"Like Alana? I've heard they say she has seizures."

"No. She's a portal guardian."

He whistled.

He was already impressed with Alana because she was a Kubiteron. Now even more so because she was a gate guardian? Ugh. It was hard not to like her though. She'd been a friend to Celeste from the beginning. Well, almost from the beginning. All demons were a little wary of all other demons.

Samson continued to walk behind them, and Wendell glanced back at him. "Don't tell me. He's the gate guardian's protector."

"Hell, yeah, except I'm here to protect Celeste for the moment," Samson said.

"If you ever heard Samson and Hunter talking about who protects Alana, you'll learn they're in disagreement," Celeste said.

Wendell smiled back at Samson.

He shrugged. "Hunter has got it wrong."

Wendell shook his head. "Okay, so I guess Hunter can't be all that bad. Not if a Samuria can disagree with a Matusa and live."

"Why are we headed this way?" Samson said. "Your classes are back that way."

"We're going to skip classes. Alana, or Hunter, is going to send Wendell home, no sense in him going to any more classes."

Wendell raised his brows, looking surprised to hear it.

"And you?" Samson asked.

"I need to learn all that I can about the demon world from someone who has been living there recently, so I'm sticking with Wendell until Alana...or Hunter sends him back."

"I have been there recently," Samson reminded her, sounding disgruntled, as if his experiences didn't count for anything. "And you still need to earn your high school diploma."

"You were living in the swamps, or at least a village near there." Celeste frowned at Wendell. "Tell me you lived near a city or know something about the Hall of Records."

"Why would you want to know that?" Wendell asked as the three of them left school.

"We're going to find our families."

"Families?"

"Yeah, sure, we're all of demon heritage. We all have family there, though we don't want to go there to live. Mostly because we've never lived there, or we've been here too long. Except for Samson. He feels he must stick with Alana. I suspect he's glad to get out of the swamps where he lived. I was just three when my summoner parents summoned me."

Samson shook his head.

"But they made the mistake of thinking they could summon a baby boy to be my brother. Instead, they summoned a full adult Matusa. He killed them, but left me alone, since I was a demon child, and had nothing to do with summoning him," Celeste said.

"So you don't know where your parents are?"

"Back in Seplichus. But where? No. Or even who they were? I haven't a clue."

Samson was texting someone.

Celeste scowled at him. "You're telling Hunter on me, aren't you?"

"You're skipping school with another demon. Sure, I'm telling Hunter what's going on. If any of them are tracking us—"

"Tracking us?" Wendell asked.

"Yeah. Jared's a whiz at making electronic gadgets. He created a small demon signature tracking device to keep an eye on where demons are appearing in our world," Celeste said.

"Yeah, which means they'll see we all left the building and might be worried you're having one of your visions and are leaping into danger," Samson said.

"I have family who live near the Hall of Records. We can stay with them once we reach there," Wendell said.

"But we can't open a portal here that will be close to there, can we?" Celeste asked.

"No, but I have an apartment in this vicinity. A train will take us to the Hall of Records."

"How long is the train ride? I can imagine having trouble all the way to the city where the Hall of Records is located, just because of Alana."

"Can we leave her behind?" Wendell asked, sounding serious.

"She wants to see her father. And Hunter won't leave her behind anyway because he believes he has to protect her."

"I have to protect her," Samson said, "so where she goes, or stays, I go...or stay."

"All right. So, where are we going now?" Wendell asked as Celeste led him to her car.

"We need to pack a bag. If we can stay with your family, that would be great."

Samson was texting away.

"I doubt my aunt and uncle would be happy to put the Matusa up."

"If it doesn't work out, we can always return to Earth world,"

Samson said. "We can go to Alana's uncle's house in Dallas. He lives near there. Then we can drop into the area when we want. I haven't been there with them, but maybe I can pinpoint where we need to open the portal so that we'll be on the steps of the building, or maybe even inside. Jared said that when you get inside, no one can cause any trouble for any demon type."

"All right. It's settled then." Celeste saw Alana, Hunter, and Jared exiting the building. "Either they've spotted another demon type, or they want to talk to you, Wendell."

Wendell stiffened his back, his gaze shifting from Alana to Hunter.

When they reached him, Alana stuck out her hand to Wendell in greeting. He glanced again at Hunter, who gave him a dark smile. Celeste knew Hunter was glad the Camaran demon was afraid of stoking his ire. At least someone was.

"Spill," Hunter said. "Tell us everything."

8

It wasn't in their nature to trust other demons, so immediately, upon learning that Wendell was a demon cloaking that he was, Hunter was suspicious. The only good thing about the guy was that he appeared to want to help them and was afraid of Hunter. All of them should be, but one out of five was a start. They swung by Wendell's foster parents' home, the parents both at work at some ad agency, and he packed a bag while they waited.

Jared said to Hunter, "Our choices are to go to the train and head for the Hall of Records that way and stay with Wendell's aunt and uncle, or I can get us on a flight out of here, land in on Alana's uncle in Dallas, and we'll portal over to the Hall of Records that way."

"Portal?" Alana asked.

"Yeah. I figure that works. Noun: portal. Verb: portal."

She shook her head.

"Can you create a portal that is closer to the Hall of Records? Maybe inside the Hall of Records?" Samson asked Jared.

"Yeah. I've correlated where we've transported before, and this is the closest place we can get. Right next to the steps." Jared pointed to a location on the map. "I'm not sure we can portal into the building."

"Then we fly from Baltimore to Dallas. Check to see if we can all fly there on the same plane," Hunter said.

Jared checked the flights. "We can make the flight out in two hours. That will give us time to grab our gear and head over there." He frowned. "Well, make that three of us can go. The rest have to take another flight. That one leaves three hours later."

"Okay, then the three of us will wait for the others to arrive." Hunter assumed everyone would know that the original team of demon hunters—him, Jared, and Alana—would go first. They would stay at her uncle's house. Hunter had to protect Alana no matter what. Jared was essential for getting everyone there in the first place.

The rest would be essential for the next phase of the plan—enter Seplichus and keep from getting into too much trouble. There was no sense in hoping they wouldn't. All they could hope for was that it wouldn't be too much for them to handle.

Hunter had considered that they go in small groups to locate family, but he believed, with their combined strengths, they would fare better if they stuck together.

"I don't like this plan," Samson said, frowning at Hunter.

"You don't have to."

"I'm texting my uncle to let him know we're landing in on him," Alana said, and Hunter knew that was her ploy to change the subject to one less volatile.

"Hey, you can protect me and Wendell," Celeste said.

Hunter knew from Samson's killing look that he wanted to guard the Kubiteron.

"Okay, I left my parents a note saying I found my family, and I'm going home to them. And thanked them for everything. That's the only regret I have. They were good to me." Wendell shouldered his backpack and led them outside. "We're going through a portal?"

"No. We'll fly out to Dallas," Hunter said. "You can leave your vehicle here."

"Why?" Wendell still looked nervous around Hunter, keeping his distance, but he looked relieved he would be returning home.

Hunter gave him a quelling look. "Alana and I'll be heading to her place to pack."

"And me," Celeste said. "But I'll drive my car."

"I'll take whoever wants to ride in my Jeep," Jared said.

"I'll go with Celeste," Wendell said.

Samson climbed into Jared's Jeep. "Alana needs to go with Celeste so she can pack. And Jared and Hunter should go together."

Hunter ignored him and drove off. He wasn't about to have Samson reorder who went with whom and where, even if it made sense. Hunter didn't trust Wendell with Alana. What if he forced her to open a portal here so he could return home and not go to his aunt and uncle's home near the Hall of Records?

Anyone that Hunter hadn't worked with for a while, was suspect.

"Samson was right, you know." Alana buckled her seat belt.

Hunter glanced at her. "You trust him completely?" He knew he sounded like he couldn't believe after they'd been through so much, that she would be that gullible.

"Of course not. He could help us, not bother to—once he gets what he wants—or turn on us. It's a gamble like it usually is."

When they dropped by Alana's place, she hurried to pack up. Celeste hadn't arrived yet. Hunter didn't like it.

Jared texted Hunter: I'm at my place.

Hunter responded: We are at Alana's home and then headed to your place.

Meet you here. Jared.

"I left some stuff at my Uncle Stephen's house, so I won't need to pack much," Alana said.

Hunter was watching out the window. "I'll text your mom to let her know we're headed out on a flight in a couple of hours."

"Thanks."

Celeste pulled up and parked her car. Hunter watched as Wendell and she got out of the car.

"They're here. If you're done here, we'll head on over to my place so I can pack, and we can pick up Jared and drive to the airport. Celeste and the others can leave when they need to for their flight."

"Okay. I'm ready." She joined Hunter at the window. "Are you trying to do your Matusa stare down on Wendell?"

Hunter smiled. "He just saw me watching him."

She took Hunter's hand. "Come on. Let's go."

They met Celeste at the door. "We'll pick you up at the airport when you arrive in Dallas," Hunter said.

"See you there."

"What took you so long to get here?" Hunter asked before they left.

"Traffic. We hit every red light."

Hunter figured that if he could do it, Wendell would have controlled the traffic lights so they wouldn't arrive until later and might even miss seeing Hunter.

"We'll see you." Alana climbed into the truck.

Hunter gave Wendell another searing look, reminding him who was in charge, just in case he caused trouble for Celeste or Samson. Then he got in his truck and drove toward his place. The apartment complex was as close as he could get to Alana's housing development, so it didn't take long before they were there.

Jared had already pulled Hunter's field pack out and had his bags ready to go. He started loading up the truck while Hunter packed his bag. Samson was sitting in the living room with his packed bag beside him.

Alana watched Hunter stuffing things into the bag.

"Do you ever fold anything neatly?"

"Everything's wrinkle resistant."

She shook her head.

Hunter grabbed his bag and headed back out to the truck. "We have just enough time to get to the airport. Samson, is Celeste picking you up when you need to leave?"

"She is."

"See you soon," Hunter said.

Then Hunter and his little party headed for the airport.

"This almost feels like old times," Jared said. "Except that Alana's with us."

"That feels like old times too," Hunter said. "I admit Celeste and Samson have helped us out a few times."

They finally parked at the airport and headed inside to make their flight.

"I wonder where Indigo is?" Alana asked. "I haven't seen him around in a while."

"Good." Hunter hadn't missed the ghostly Matusa. "You want the window seat this time, don't you?" Hunter asked Alana as they boarded the plane.

"Sure."

Jared snorted. "You know you don't have to worry about me with Alana."

"It's a Matusa thing," Alana said. "Get used to it."

"I've had to get used to a lot of things over the years. I just never expected to see Hunter stuck on a girl."

"Not any girl," Alana said.

"No, a Kubiteron. Don't you ever feel that's the only reason he has the hots for you? That it has nothing to do with you personally?"

Hunter gave him a look that said to cease asking the questions. He'd never shown any interest in anyone but Alana. Not when he was half demon. How could a human girl deal with that? He would have to keep his demon heritage and occupation a secret. He'd seen several Kubiteron over the years while he'd been trying to send them home, so it wasn't like any Kubiteron female would do.

"He adores me for being me." Alana fastened her seatbelt.

"Maybe it's your witchy half then." Jared fastened his seatbelt.

The pilot said over the intercom, "We're flying to Shreveport, Louisiana in just a few minutes."

Everyone on the plane looked at everyone else.

Then the pilot added, "After a stopover in Dallas."

Several passengers laughed. Not Hunter.

Alana took his hand and squeezed. "You have to admit the pilot has our kind of humor." She glanced across at Hunter to see Jared putting his phone away. "You were checking to see if we were on the wrong flight?"

"Of course not." Jared sounded defensive enough that Hunter suspected he had been.

"Okay, my uncle wasn't home, and he's not answering his text messages." Alana tucked her phone away.

As soon as the plane took off, the air chilled so many degrees that Hunter knew Indigo was with them.

"Can Indigo go through the portal when we open it?" Hunter wondered if he could get rid of him that way.

"Maybe. Or he might need to be more than his ghostly state to do it." Alana snuggled closer to Hunter.

That was one good thing about Indigo's chilling effect. Alana always got closer to Hunter to get warmed up when Indigo hassled them.

"Can we still get into your uncle's place, even if he's not at home?" Hunter asked.

"We can, as long as he hasn't erected any new barriers that I don't know about to keep others out."

"Would he?"

"He might. I texted Mom to let her know I couldn't reach him.

She said she would keep trying too. He might have gone to a warlock convention or conference. Hopefully, we'll be able to get into the house without any trouble."

"If he erects a barrier, can it electrocute us?" Jared asked.

"No telling what he might put in place," Alana said.

"How do you think he'll feel about a whole passel of demons landing in on him?" Jared asked. "Should I book a couple of rooms at a hotel?"

"Yeah," Hunter said. "Good idea. Just in case, and we can always cancel the reservations if we don't need them." He turned to Alana. "Did you pack your frog prince pajamas?"

"Did you pack your red-hot chili peppers boxers?" she asked.

Jared chuckled.

"I need to stop in on my human parents when we have time," Hunter said. He loved his adoptive parents and his younger sister. He didn't want them to feel as though they'd raised him, and then he had abandoned them. Particularly, after he'd learned of his real mother and father.

"You need to have Alana wipe away any knowledge that you exist," Jared said.

Hunter gave him a growly look.

"Or not. It would just make it easier."

"Do you want me to do that to your adoptive parents, Jared?" Alana asked.

"Of course not. They pay for all our accommodations."

Alana shook her head. "It's more than that."

"Yes. I love them. I rarely see them, but I care for them."

"Okay. So, Hunter cares for his family too."

"Not Bentos," Hunter said.

"Your demon father too," Alana corrected him. "He saved your life. For that, you're grateful, even if you don't want to admit it. And he didn't kill your human mother when she summoned him."

"He won't tell me where my half-brother is."

"He probably thinks he's not ready to learn about his demon heritage. Look how hard it was for us to learn of it."

"Bentos prefers his mom to my mom. He broke my mother's heart."

"He's a Matusa."

"Yeah, and he wants you. Don't ever forget that part." Hunter couldn't help the antagonism he felt for his dad. He couldn't forgive him for breaking his mother's heart, though Hunter knew deep down that his dad leaving her had been the best thing that could have happened for her. But the business with his father wanting Alana? That's where Hunter drew the line. The problem was he still couldn't fully claim her until they were married. That meant other Matusa believed she was fair game.

"We have to get married."

"What?" she asked, her green eyes wide.

Hunter wasn't going to get down on bended knee and ask. She was his and there were no two ways about it. He figured she would give him grief over the way he gave her the news. He welcomed it.

Jared laughed. "Way to go, Hunter. If that was a proposal of marriage, it sucked."

"Look up in your notes on the proper etiquette for a Matusa taking a Kubiteron for a mate." Hunter was sure Jared wouldn't have any.

"She's witchy too." Jared looked at his notepad. "It says here the Matusa beats his chest, then throws the Kubiteron over his shoulder, and hauls her off to his cave."

Hunter smiled at Alana.

She folded her arms, brows raised. "Jared's pulling your leg. I'm the one who beats on your chest."

The guys both chuckled.

Jared ran his finger over his notes and said, "Right."

"But it doesn't mean I'm saying I do," she said. "If you think you'll get rid of the other Matusa who are interested in me, you'll have to come up with an alternate plan."

"We could leave you behind," Jared said, serious as could be. "For your safety."

"I'm not marrying anyone until I finish a bachelor's degree."

"That's going to be never if you keep skipping classes or missing them because of your astral traveling. As soon as you graduate from high school, I'm marrying you. No argument. Your mother said she was all for it because she knows I'm the only one who can protect you."

Hunter sighed. He would have this his way, the only way he could protect her.

"Your uncle agreed. And your dad even said yes. The day after your high school graduation, we do it." Hunter studied Alana's expression, but she looked...*expressionless*. "Alana?" He shook her shoulder. "Hell, she's...gone. Where did we just fly over?"

Jared was already looking up the flight route. "Memphis, Tennessee. She can't have been pulled to a portal. Wouldn't the fall from the airplane kill her?"

"She's astral traveling. I can't believe this."

"You still want to marry her?"

"Where were we when she left her body?" Hunter was searching for demon signatures, but except for the three of them on the plane, he saw no others. "You need to extend the distance on these." He was so frustrated that he growled the words.

"Thirty-nine-thousand feet? I'll get right on it. *Not*."

"If I could stop the plane, I would," Hunter said. They would never reach her quickly enough.

"I can." Jared got on his computer and hacked into the plane's computer system. The plane flew a short distance and then began to turn back toward the airport in Memphis. "We just need to wait for them to get clearance."

"You are sure handy to have around."

"Thanks." Jared sounded proud of his efforts. "What about Alana?"

"Federal agents are sure to be on the ground, checking us all out. If we're lucky, Alana will return to us from her astral traveling. Otherwise, we'll have to tell them she has got epilepsy and having one of her episodes."

When they landed, federal agents met the plane and detained everyone, looking for someone who had misdirected the flight electronically. Hunter was trying not to look anxious, which could indicate he'd had something to do with this. He had to restrain himself from looking at the demon tracker. He was desperate to find Alana. For now, he had his arm wrapped around Alana's physical form.

"On drugs?" one of the feds asked Hunter.

"She has seizures. I think she was upset about the plane turning away from our destination. We're going to take a car to Dallas instead of flying the rest of the way, and hope she is more herself soon." Hunter showed the agent her medication that she always carried with her, just to prove she wasn't faking this. He released them, wishing them a safe journey.

Once the feds couldn't find any evidence onboard that showed a passenger had done it, the plane was taken out of service for a more thorough examination.

"Come on, Jared." While other passengers from the flight were scrambling to find other flights to take to Dallas, Hunter was checking out the demon tracker. "The demon signature is this way —a Kubiteron and a Samuria about a mile east of here. We'll pick up a rental car and drive the rest of the way to Dallas. I always thought she would be safe from the opening of portals when she's flying that far away."

"Yeah me too, but you know it could be her abilities are evolving."

"Being more sensitive to the pull of a portal isn't evolving. It's a disaster. Evolving would mean she'd have some control over being pulled to them."

"I agree. So she has become more powerful, in one respect? Or the portals are?"

"I don't know." Hunter frowned at the tracker as they headed for the rental car counter, his arm around Alana's waist, trying to move her quickly, while Jared carried his bag and Alana's. "I hope this Samuria isn't like Samson. We don't need another one thinking he's Alana's guardian."

They had to grab a bus to the rental car lot and when they arrived there, they hurried to get their car. They threw their bags in the car, and Hunter helped Alana into the back seat, then buckled her in. "We're getting married when you graduate."

Jared chuckled. "It's easier to convince her of that when she's not all here."

Then Hunter jumped into the driver's seat while Jared climbed into the passenger's seat and directed them to the site where Alana's astral version self was. "They haven't moved," Jared said.

"Yeah, I don't know why she hasn't sent him back to the demon world."

"Unless he's like us and has lived here always."

"Or he's like Samson and believes he's now here to protect the gate guardian."

"There she is." Jared pointed to her and a redheaded guy standing at a convenience store.

As soon as they parked as close as they could get and climbed out of the vehicle, the Samuria pulled Alana behind him, as if protecting her from Hunter.

"We're Alana's friends," Hunter said.

"He's right." Alana vanished and the car door opened. Alana stepped out.

"You're back," Jared said.

"Yeah. That was one unbelievable ride."

"As long as you're safe." Hunter glanced around and didn't see any people nearby. He opened a portal and said to the Samuria. "Go. Return to your world."

"I'm the gate guardian's guard."

"No, you're not."

"I tried explaining this to him. Samson is, but Samson isn't here protecting me, so this guy doesn't believe me," Alana said.

"Where's your summoner?" Hunter asked.

"Dead," Alana answered for him. "This is really not the place to hang around."

"All right, go then," Hunter said to the Samuria. "You are a full demon, and just recently brought over, right?"

"Yeah, but—"

"Sorry, dude, but it's not happening." Hunter knew what the Samuria was going to say before he said it. He'd laid claim to be Alana's guard. Hunter shoved the guy through the portal and closed it. He didn't want anything else entering their world, and he wouldn't stand around arguing all day with the guy. Then he saw a gang of young men who looked to be trouble. At least, they gave the impression that Hunter, Alana, and Jared had been ordinary humans.

The men were wearing knives, chains, and their whole-body postures saying this was their territory, and Hunter and his friends didn't belong there. And they were leaning against their rental car. They hadn't even heard them arrive.

"Can you do something with these guys?" Hunter asked Alana. "My choice would be heart seizure, fireballs, or send them to the demon world. But you might be able to do something that isn't quite so lethal."

"Wrap us in a protection spell? No way." She opened a portal and then blasted them with a tornado-strength force of wind that pushed four of them into it. She elevated two more and sent them through. Three others were staring at the light and where their friends had gone. "Your choice. Either you take off running, or you end up in a black hole."

One aimed to shoot her, and Hunter tossed him into the portal. She didn't hesitate to sweep the other two up, using her levitation spell again, and moved them into the portal, and closed it. A few other guys had shown up and were watching from a distance. But no one else approached.

She wiped her hands together, as if brushing off the dirt she'd just handled. "Now where to?" She climbed into the car.

Hunter and Jared cast looks at each other, then climbed into the car, and Hunter tore off.

"We're driving to Dallas. I'm not risking that you'll be pulled to another portal while we're flying."

"I thought you were going to do something less lethal than Hunter was aiming to do," Jared said.

Hunter chuckled. "That's why I'm marrying her after she graduates from high school. She's my kind of demon. And if she doesn't finish high school, she's going to earn her GED."

"Good. One senior year of high school was enough for me," Jared said, though he'd already enrolled in college courses online through Georgia Tech.

"*After* college, you mean," Alana said. "And that *was* less lethal than giving them all heart attacks or shooting fireballs at them. However, once they arrive in the demon world, they won't be so tough. I would almost like to see how they handle their stay there, for as long as they live."

"Have you ever thought of the consequences of us dumping our garbage on the demon world?" Jared asked.

"Okay, you're right," Alana said. "Should we rescue them and send them back to our world so they can continue to threaten innocent people?"

"No," Hunter said, "but Jared's right. Still, I would love to have seen their faces when they realized they're in a world where the Matusa can make short work of them. I doubt they'll be all that tough then."

"Other demon kind can take them out too," Jared reminded him. "Though we may be lower in strength than your kind, we can do some real damage. We might be afraid of the Matusa, but not so much of humans like that. Not if they have weapons they threaten us with. And you know they will threaten them."

"True. At this rate, we won't make it to your uncle's home until well after the rest of our group reaches Dallas," Hunter said. "We have six and half hours to drive to get there."

"Not the way you're speeding. What would you do if I couldn't control a police officer's mind if one stopped you for speeding? Slow it down so we can get there in one piece. I still can't get ahold of my uncle anyway. The others will have to go to a hotel until we reach Dallas."

"I'll text them," Jared said.

"We should have waited two more days before spring break," Hunter said, "and left on Friday after school, like we planned."

"You know you couldn't wait for this any more than we could. Besides, this is our job. To return demons to their home. And Wendell needs to go home."

"We could have waited two days."

"I think you secretly like him because he's afraid of you when no one else is. Must be your human half." Alana smiled at Hunter.

He grunted. "Are you still trying to get ahold of your uncle?"

"Yeah, I'll try again." She shook her head. "Nothing."

He glanced at her.

"He takes off like this from time to time so he can concentrate on conjuring up new skills."

◦~

THREE HOURS INTO THEIR JOURNEY, Jared was asleep in the back.

Alana glanced back at him. "I sure hope if we find his parents, he's not disappointed. What if he wants to stay with them?"

"I doubt he would. He enjoys being in our world. He loves his human family."

"He loves helping you," Alana said.

"Yeah, and though he won't admit it, he loves helping you too."

Alana got a call from Celeste. "Putting it on speaker. Hey, Celeste, where are you?"

"We just checked into the hotel. Where are you?"

"Halfway there. How's Wendell?"

"He's fine. Samson's pissed though. He wanted to be with you."

"Don't tell him that another Samuria wanted to be my protector."

Celeste laughed. "I won't. I imagine Hunter got rid of him fast enough."

"Yep. Sent him through a portal. Get some lunch. We'll get there when we can. We don't want to have to eat in Seplichus," Alana said. "We'll have to pop into our world from time to time to get something to eat. We'll call you when we're close to Dallas."

"Okay, well, no more detours for you."

"I sure hope not. At least I don't plan to."

"I can't believe you did that."

"Neither can I."

"Okay, we're having lunch. Samson said to hurry it up and no more portal diversions."

"I hope she can avoid them," Hunter said.

THREE HOURS LATER, they arrived in Dallas and met at the hotel where everyone was staying. "Are you ready for this?" Hunter asked.

Wendell agreed.

"Okay, let's do it."

9

Hunter had decided that he could find his half-brother later. He wanted Alana to find her father, and Jared to locate his parents first. Celeste also. At least Samson didn't need to find anyone. He was just stuck on Alana.

As soon as they arrived near the Hall of Records, Wendell gave them directions to his aunt and uncle's house, thanked them for bringing him there, and took off. Hunter wondered if the kid gave them good directions to his family's home or not—afraid to tell his relatives a Matusa might be coming to dinner. He did appear grateful they had brought him home, and Hunter was glad for that.

The rest of them hurried up the steps before Alana caught a bunch of demons' attention.

Inside, they met up with Treikal, the records custodian, a ruling prince's cousin, and the reason he had such an important job. Jared was supposedly distantly related to Treikal also.

Treikal smiled at Jared. "You have come back to search for your family?"

"Yes, and Alana's dad's location. He's a gate guardian. Pappalios."

"He should be easy to find."

They followed Treikal down the black marble walk to the records room where they would search for their families.

On the computer, Treikal pulled up the record on Pappalios and inclined his head to Alana so she could contact her dad. "Good luck," Treikal said and left them in peace.

Alana took a seat at the computer and glanced up at Hunter as he watched what she was doing. "I thought you were going to look for your dad to see if there's any record of you and your half-brother here."

"I would prefer to help you find your dad for now." Hunter glanced at Jared, who was concentrating hard on what he was doing on the computer next to them. "Find anything?"

"Yeah, I think this might be my uncle. He's close by. I could run over there and see him."

"We'll go with you," Hunter said, but when Jared looked up at him, seeming surprised, Hunter thought maybe he was butting in where he wasn't wanted. Still, he'd always had it in mind that he would accompany Jared when he found his family. He didn't want him to get into any trouble. And if his family wanted to keep him in the demon world, Hunter wanted to make sure it was Jared's choice.

"Yeah, sure, but he might not like that you're a Matusa. Just saying."

Hunter was glad that was Jared's only concern. His family would have to deal with it.

"Hey, Dad," Alana said, sounding excited when she was able to get ahold of her dad on the on-view screen. "We're here!"

"What are you doing at the Hall of Records?" her dad asked, looking worried.

"Trying to find you."

"Is anything wrong with your mother?"

"No, no, she's fine. I'm on spring break, well, a couple of days early."

"I thought you weren't coming until the summer, for a couple of months, after you graduated from high school."

"I couldn't wait. And it's a good thing too. You have to teach me how to get this portal business under control. We were flying to Dallas, and I ended up being drawn to a portal!"

"Flying?"

"Yeah, in a plane. And we were at, like, I don't know, 40,000 feet, or something. Has that happened to you before?"

"I don't often fly in planes, but no. Is Hunter with you?" Her dad sounded concerned.

Hoping Pappalios would know how to stop her from astral traveling when they were flying, Hunter moved closer so that her dad could see him. Her dad was a blond like Alana, with the same sea-green eyes, and the same pleasing smile.

"Yes, sir. However I have to admit, Alana and I are at an impasse. She wants to wait until she graduates from college to marry me. I say we get hitched right after she graduates from high school." He hoped her dad would convince her that she would be safer if they were married.

"Don't delay," her dad said.

Hunter smiled. He really liked her dad. "That's what I say."

He wasn't sure if her mom would agree with him or would want to leave it up to Alana. Yes, they were young, but they weren't like regular teens. Between being half-demons, and Alana being half-witch, they were well-matched in talents for dealing with the deadly Matusa.

And though he would like to say he was the one always responsible for saving her life, she'd saved him a few times too. He didn't like to admit that he couldn't live without her, or that she was always on his mind when they were apart. They were meant to be together. Waiting four more years wasn't going to change that.

Her dad began giving them directions to his place. "Take the train that's near the Hall of Records to East End. It'll take an hour. Just let me know when you get a ticket."

"Okay, Jared's located an uncle, so he's nearby, and we'll see him first. Celeste is still looking to see if she can find any of her kin. She was only three when she ended up in Earth world," Alana said.

"All right. Just make sure Hunter is with you at all times," her dad said.

"And me," Samson said, peering down at the computer screen.

"The Samuria. Of course. I'll expect you for dinner unless you specify otherwise."

"Demon food?" Alana asked.

"As a portal guardian, I can return to your world when I want. I stocked up on plenty of goodies. Human goodies. I've gotten used to a lot of the foods. Steak, in particular."

"Okay, great. Is it safe for us to travel and to stay at your place?" Alana asked.

"As long as Hunter is with you at all times. I had some rings made for you to wear that will indicate Hunter has claimed you for his own."

Alana tilted her chin down in a way that said she didn't care for the idea that anyone had claimed her. Hunter couldn't help smiling at her. Sure, it wasn't that way in the human world, but in the demon world, rank had its privileges. Not that he would even consider claiming her for his mate if he wasn't sure she was the one he wanted to be with always. But he did like that he got to do the claiming...in this world.

"He's a Matusa," her dad reminded her. "And will keep you safe."

"I will keep her safe," Samson said.

Hunter grunted, but then took Alana's hand and gave her a smirk.

"Okay, see you soon. Love you," her dad said.

Alana smiled at her dad. "Love you too, Dad. As soon as we

have tickets and know for sure when we'll be arriving, we'll come back here and let you know."

"Good show."

Then she signed off. She looked up at Hunter, and he thought she was going to give him grief about claiming her, though when she beat on his chest to bring him back to life, he knew she had claimed him right back. Instead, she said, "Are you sure you don't want to see if you can learn anything about your half-brother?"

"No. We have too many others we're looking for this trip. And... maybe my dad's right. Maybe my brother isn't ready to learn about his demon heritage."

Jared was on the screen talking with a man who resembled him, and Hunter was glad he'd finally found one of his kin. He'd been looking for so long. "Okay, thanks, Uncle. I'll be bringing some of my friends if it's all right with you. Hunter's a half Matusa, half human, but we've been friends for years."

His uncle didn't look pleased to hear it, but Jared continued, "He has saved my life numerous times. He's not one of the bad ones. Believe me."

"All right." But his uncle looked skeptical.

"We'll see you soon. We just have a Camaran friend who's looking for her family."

His uncle frowned. "You've all been living in the human world?"

"Yeah. Do you know what happened to my parents?"

"I do, but we'll talk when you get here."

"All right." Then Jared signed off, but his expression had turned dark.

"It won't be bad news," Hunter said, though he didn't know the truth, and he shouldn't have speculated.

Jared shook his head. "Don't you think he would have said if it was good news? That they lived near him?"

"We'll just see what he has to say," Alana said. "No sense in thinking up bad scenarios to explain it."

They turned their attention to Celeste. She was wiping tears off her face.

Alana hurried over to her and rubbed her back. "What's wrong?"

Celeste hesitated to say. Then she finally shut down the computer. "I couldn't find anyone."

Hunter wondered if something else was bothering her. Still, both Alana and Jared had found someone, so she could feel bad that she was the only one who hadn't.

"Do you want to go with us? Or do you want me to open the portal so you can return to the hotel in Dallas until we're done?" Hunter asked.

"I have to stay here."

"Okay." Hunter felt uneasy about her declaration. Not that she wanted to stay with them, but that she *had* to stay here. Not even particularly *with* them. He didn't want to lose her in the demon world. She had never indicated she'd wanted to stay here for any length of time.

So what else was the matter? Her psychic visions instantly came to mind.

CELESTE HATED it when she had a vision, especially when she was so keen on learning if she had any other family. Not that she wanted to live with them, but she wanted to know, like Jared did, how she had ended up in the human world. Jared's adoptive parents were the greatest.

Her foster parents had been too worried about her uncanny sense of knowing future events. She couldn't help it. If she could aid someone by knowing what could occur, she had to warn the person. She also understood—to an extent—how that would freak them out.

She was glad Alana's mother had taken her in, and Celeste didn't have to worry about how she felt about it. Alana's mother was a ghostbuster and a witch, so the unusual didn't faze her in the least. It was good knowing Celeste could be different and accepted for who she was.

She did wonder if her real parents had the same talent as she did. Or someone else in the family tree had the ability. She glanced back at Hunter. She was certain he knew something was going on with her, but he was allowing her to be the one who mentioned it first. She appreciated him for it.

"It's snowing outside. A blizzard, really," Celeste said as they left the computer room and headed down the long corridor to the outside world.

Hunter glanced at her.

"Yeah, I saw it in a vision. So maybe it isn't starting right now. Or maybe it won't start for a while."

"And?" Hunter asked, frowning.

"There's going to be a train wreck." This was when she hated the visions. Not knowing how to deal with it. How could she control anything that would help to change the outcome?

"*And?*" Hunter persisted, slowing his pace and eyeing her with suspicion.

"I don't know."

"That's why you were crying?"

"We lose each other, okay? In the snow, the blizzard, the pile of train cars derailed. I don't know all the specifics."

"So we don't take the train," Hunter said.

"I don't know. If we didn't, then would I be seeing this in my mind's eye?"

Pulling Celeste to a stop, Hunter growled. "We've had this discussion before. Sometimes, you can't change anything and what will happen...happens. Other times, you can. Do you ever have a vision where you see the future one way, and then you see a new future vision and things have changed because you've altered the direction you were headed?"

"No. I don't see them all the time. Only when something catastrophic seems to be headed my way."

"And if you altered your plans, do you ever truly change the outcome?"

"Yes. Sometimes. I can't say that it's a better outcome though." Celeste hated that she couldn't give Hunter better news, but that was the problem with having future visions.

"Then we don't take the train," Alana said. "Simple as that."

"When will this occur?" Hunter asked.

"I don't know. It could even be while we're taking the train back here. Or at some other time, but soon. I don't have future visions of happenings that occur too far into the future."

"What if we leave Jared off with his uncle to visit, and then we take the train to see Alana's dad? That way we don't delay our trip —like we'd planned. You could even stay with Jared so we're assured not all of us will be on the train. I would leave Samson behind too, but..."

"I'm going with Alana." Samson shoved his hands in his pockets, his eyes narrowed as he gave Hunter a caustic look.

"Right."

"But...what if, by us changing what we do—we go early, Jared and Celeste stay behind, that's why she sees the train wreck, and our not being together any longer?" Alana asked.

Hunter looked at Celeste to see her take on it.

"It could be. It's not an exact science. I see bits and pieces."

"Okay, so the question is, what do you do about it?" Jared asked.

"What do you mean by what do I do about it?" Celeste frowned at him as if he thought she could wave a magic wand and change the outcome.

"I mean, you're a Camaran demon. You are drawn to danger. I

doubt if the train was derailed, you would do nothing. What do you do?"

"I would look for everyone, of course. If I could." She thought that was a given. Except there was one little problem with that. She was pinned under the train in her vision. "Hey, if I lose Hunter or Alana, or both of them, I'm stuck here. The same as you and Samson are, you know. Only they can open the portals. So, of course, I would look for them. Frantically. If I could."

"And?" Hunter asked.

"*And...what*?" Celeste asked, throwing up her hands in exasperation.

"You don't see anyone? You haven't located anyone? You're alone?"

"I'm not alone. There are dozens of demons screaming in pain. Some, I'm sure, will die."

Hunter released his breath. "But you don't see any of us."

"It's a whiteout. I can barely make out the train." Celeste didn't realize what a hassle it would be to have psychic abilities and share them with people who believed in her. They were so clueless, that it was impossible to get the point across that her visions were vague, not so detailed that they would know when, where, and why things happened the way they did.

"You're on the train?" Alana asked.

"I'm off it. I don't know if it's because I was on it and it crashed, or because I was nearby and saw it."

"Which you couldn't do because it's a whiteout," Hunter reminded her.

"True." Celeste folded her arms. "Okay, so maybe I don't look for anyone," she admitted. "It's...worse. I'm pinned beneath the wreckage and in terrible pain." She hadn't wanted them to change their plans because of her.

"*That's* why you were crying," Hunter said.

Celeste scowled at the Matusa. As if she would cry over something like that. "I thought...I would never see you again." Then she quickly amended her statement. "Alana, the others." She motioned to them, leaving Hunter out of it.

He gave her a dark smile. "And me."

"That I would be stuck here."

"I think we should send you back to Dallas, Celeste, to keep you out of harm's way," Hunter said.

Celeste considered the notion for a second, then shook her head. "I want to be there for all of you."

"You said you are pinned beneath the train!" Hunter ran his hands through his hair, looking exasperated. "Okay, maybe we should all just go home."

"No, I want to see my uncle," Jared said.

"I want to see my dad." Alana frowned. "If we're going to be here for a while, it might be another day, not even today. I say we stick together. It was sunny out, cold, but it wasn't snowing when we arrived."

"All right," Hunter said, then looked to see Celeste's take on it.

"All right." Celeste hoped this wouldn't be a disaster, but she didn't want to return to Earth world and have to tell Alana's mother that her daughter had been lost in a train wreck in Seplichus, when she knew about it, and left Alana behind, just to keep herself safe.

They again headed for the doors to the Hall of Records and saw two Elantus demons enter, brushing snow off their parkas, and stomping their boots on a rug.

"Man, freak weather."

They glanced at Celeste and her party and frowned. "It's cold out there. You better not be traveling that far in this whiteout, dressed only like that."

Everyone looked at Celeste, and she let out her breath. "Okay, so should we, uhm, return to...you know where, and pick up some winter clothes first?"

"Yeah, we'd better." Hunter waited for the men to enter the computer room, then he opened a portal. "Let's go."

They ended up by their hotel, and he quickly closed the portal. Then they piled into the rental car, and Alana directed him to the nearest shopping mall.

"I should have let my uncle know we were going to be delayed," Jared said.

"Let's just hurry. I should have done the same with my dad, but I'm sure he would realize we were delayed for some reason. Celeste and I'll go to the junior's department. You guys can stick together."

Samson was going to object, but Hunter said, "Unless you want to stay here, or freeze to death because you didn't bother to shop for warm clothes, then you'll come with Jared and me."

Samson glanced at Alana, and she smiled, motioning for him to stay with them. Then Celeste and she hurried off to find warm clothes for their next adventure.

"Do you ever get tired of all the guys from the demon world being attracted to you because you're a Kubiteron?" Celeste asked Alana.

"Nope. No one was interested in me in school until I met up with our kind. Well, sort of our kind." Alana began trying on coats and found a warm, white parka, but Celeste shook her head.

Celeste tugged at brightly colored coats. "We'll never find you if you're dressed in white in a whiteout."

———

10

A lana found a bright pink coat, something she would probably never wear again, but she figured it was better to be safe than sorry if the others could see her wearing it.

"Better." Celeste found a bright purple coat.

Then they shopped for hats, gloves, and leggings, to wear under their jeans and boots. Everything was on huge spring discounts because Dallas's cold weather wouldn't last long.

When they were done, Alana used her witch's skills to tell the clerk they'd paid for them. Though she'd also handed her a library card, to make it appear to others waiting in line that she was using her credit card.

Then she and Celeste found the guys in the men's department picking out dull gray winter parkas.

"Bright colors, guys," Alana said. "Otherwise, we'll lose sight of you."

Samson obediently picked out a bright blue ski jacket. Jared found a red and blue one that was nice and colorful. Hunter was balking at picking out anything showy. Alana pulled out a bright green one. He shook his head. Then an orange. Same result. She showed him a bright yellow.

"I would look like a banana."

Everyone snickered.

"You can't wear gray, blue-gray, or black. Dull colors. We need you to wear something bright so that you will stand out against the snow."

"What did you get?"

Alana showed him her pink coat.

He shook his head. Then he grabbed an aqua coat. "You find one to match mine, and I'll get this one."

"The things I do for you." She and Celeste trudged back up to the junior's section and found an aqua coat, not the same color exactly, but close enough, and exchanged the pink one with that. She would wear this one again.

Jared had paid for the guy's clothes, using his parents' hefty allowance.

Then they drove back to the hotel and entered one of their rooms. They removed price tags on all the items and began dressing in warmer clothes.

"We stick together," Alana said, feeling way overdressed for the Dallas spring weather as she stood in the hotel room watching the guys pull on their boots.

"Right," Hunter said.

She thought he looked cute in his aqua parka that matched hers so well.

"We're going to stand out, you know," Jared said.

"That's the point. We can see each other in the snow," Celeste said.

"I mean, among the demons. They're going to notice us," Jared clarified.

"They always stand out," Samson said, waving at Alana and

Hunter. "Even if they wore white, the other demons would notice them."

"Is everyone ready to go?" Hunter asked.

Everyone agreed. Hunter opened a portal, and they all looked at the green and blue lights for a minute, before stepping into the demon world, and into the Hall of Records. Now, they looked like they were ready to brave the cold. Luckily, no one was in the corridor when they opened the portal. Hunter shut the portal.

"Let's go." Hunter took Alana's hand, and she swore he was more worried about her than he'd ever been.

Alana said to him, "Celeste says she loses sight of the rest of us, but it doesn't mean the rest of us lose sight of each other."

Celeste agreed.

"I hadn't thought of that." Hunter looked somewhat relieved.

Then they were hurrying down the street in the blinding snow, following the directions that Jared's uncle had given him, sticking close together, so they wouldn't lose each other in the maelstrom of a winter storm.

"Should be here," Jared said.

"But?" Hunter said.

"The house number isn't right. There's no other house in the vicinity with the same number he gave me."

"You don't think your uncle was afraid to give you the right number because you were bringing me, do you?" Hunter asked.

"He did give it to me *after* I mentioned you were coming with me."

Out of the white mist of snow, they saw a demon materialize— Wendell. "Hey, I was headed over to the Hall of Records to see what you discovered. But...you're here. Wearing winter clothes."

"Luckily, Celeste was able to tell us that a winter storm was coming," Hunter said.

"I borrowed some of my uncle's winter clothes," Wendell said.

Alana hadn't thought the Camaran demon would seek them out. She figured once they'd brought him safely here, he would run off and they would never see him again.

"My aunt and uncle wanted to invite you to dinner."

"We're going to see my dad for dinner," Alana said, "but Jared's uncle is supposed to live around here. He gave him the wrong house number though."

Wendell looked at the name and the house number. "Great! He lives four doors down from us. I'll show you the way. I wonder why he gave you the wrong house number." He glanced at Hunter as if believing he was the reason.

Alana didn't want Jared's uncle to fear Hunter, which is why she thought it was best if they stuck together and saw him.

"Hey, I'll let them know Celeste saved me and promised to bring me home, but only Hunter and Alana could do it. That way they'll know you are all right," Wendell said.

Alana was glad that Wendell had come to help them out. Jared was glum about his uncle not giving him the correct house number.

Wendell knocked on the door, and a dark-haired man answered it. He first looked at Wendell, because he was so close to the door, but he immediately glanced at Hunter and Alana, then surveyed the others.

"I'm Jared," Jared said, "your nephew."

His uncle inclined his head in greeting.

"I'm Wendell and my aunt and uncle live a few doors down from you. They saved me." Wendell motioned to the gathered group. "And returned me home to our world. Without their help, I would have been dead."

"What if the Matusa is forcing you to say this?" Jared's uncle cast Hunter a wary look.

"Why would he?" Alana asked. "He's half human, and so am I, which is part of the reason we can open a portal, but also, I'm a gate guardian. Jared has been searching the Hall of Records for a couple of years, looking for any sign of his family. Can you help us? Or not?"

He opened the door wider to allow them entry.

"Thank you," Alana said, shivering. She wasn't used to this cold, and she didn't want to stand out in it any longer than necessary. She was glad that Jared's uncle finally let them in.

He led them into a living room where he had a warm fire going. Nobody else appeared to be here, and she wondered if he had a mate, or had lost one.

They began removing coats, hats, and gloves and piled them on a chair, then everyone took a seat in the living room.

"I would offer some of my wine, but it's a demon brand, and you might not be able to handle it."

"No, I'm fine, thank you. We're going to my dad's place for dinner," Alana said. "He's also a gate guardian, but we have to take the train to get there. Though it might not run with this storm raging like this."

"It always runs, no matter the weather. Jared, your parents, my brother, and his mate, were summoned into Earth world. You weren't even born yet. You must have been born there. I didn't know they were going to have a son. We were having a birthday celebration for my brother and me. Your mom and dad were holding hands, leaning over to kiss each other."

Jared frowned.

"Suddenly, the blue and green lights were there, and then they were gone. Your parents, the lights, all of it. We knew what it meant. We cursed the summoner who had done it, wishing that he, or she, had summoned a Matusa and the demon killed the summoner for it instead of ripping our family apart. I had no hope to ever see them again."

"My parents are in Earth world?" Jared asked, hopeful.

That wouldn't explain why he'd been adopted by a childless human couple, Alana thought morosely.

"As far as I know. Unless they're dead at the hands of their summoner."

Jared quickly said, "Were they taken from here?"

Which would mean they could be in the Dallas area.

"No, West End. The stop before Porto, the storm city. I can give you directions to their old home. Another family lives there now. I kept it for them for three years, but I knew it was futile. That they would never find their way back. The money from the proceeds of the house is in a bank account set aside for them if they ever returned."

Jared looked at Hunter. "I want to go there now."

"Do you want me to open a portal to Earth world there so you can see where the portal leads?" Hunter asked.

"Yes. What if they've been there all along? Wherever 'there' is. I want to go there now."

But Alana wanted to see her dad.

"My aunt and uncle still want to thank you for saving my life," Wendell said.

"Will you come back to see me? Whether or not you find my brother and sister-in-law?" Jared's uncle asked.

"Yes." Jared gave his uncle a hug, tears in his eyes. "I will. I'll be back. Hopefully, to return to my parents' home."

Alana considered Hunter's expression. He was frowning, but she was certain that he wanted the best for his friend. And if that meant living in the demon world with his real family, he would let him go.

It wouldn't be easy, as close as they were to each other.

"Let's see Wendell's aunt and uncle, and then we'll take Jared to the West End," Hunter said.

"I could see my dad, while you do that." She was thinking Hunter might want some time alone with his best friend.

Everyone said, "No!"

Even Jared's uncle. "You would never reach your dad's house without Hunter by your side," Jared's uncle said. "He must go with you."

"Did you want to come with me?" Jared asked his uncle.

His uncle gave a bitter laugh. "Not in a million years."

Then they said their goodbyes, promising to bring Jared back when he was ready to see his uncle again and headed over to Wendell's family's home.

"We'll find them," Alana said, hoping they would.

"Have you had any more premonitions?" Hunter asked Celeste.

She shook her head. "If Jared wants to spend his spring break in Earth world, I'll help him."

Hunter looked at Samson.

"I'm Alana's bodyguard."

Hunter let his breath out as they kept together in the veil of snowfall and continued to Wendell's family's home.

"We'll take Jared and Celeste to West End and open a portal there. We'll all go through to ensure it's a location that you can navigate all right. Not in the middle of nowhere, or something. Then the rest of us will take the train back to East End where Alana's dad lives," Hunter said.

"I'll go with you," Wendell said. "Not that I want to go back to Earth world, but I'll help Alana get back to her dad, and my parents live in that direction."

"Does anyone remember the part about the train derailment?" Celeste asked.

"Train derailment?" Wendell asked, brows raised.

"She's psychic. Wait, you're a Camaran demon too," Jared said. "Are you psychic?"

"Yeah, but I don't see everything that's going to happen. You see the train derail?" Wendell asked Celeste.

"Yeah, in a blizzard like this one."

"We've never had a train derail before."

"If you come with us, Wendell, and you're involved in it, could you see a vision of it?" Alana asked, hopeful that if he could, but hadn't, it meant that if they went with him, it wouldn't happen.

"Not always, no."

They arrived at Wendell's family's home, and he knocked on the door. When a man and woman answered, Wendell introduced them to his family. They were gracious, wary of Hunter, which was always normal, but thankful that they'd brought him home.

"We're so grateful to you for bringing him back to us," the uncle said.

"I'm going to ride the train home," Wendell said, "so I can let Mom and Dad know I'm fine. Celeste believes she's going to be in a train derailment, however. I don't see any vision of it. Do either of you?"

"No, Wendell. Then again, if it doesn't involve us, we might not see it. Your parents will be thrilled to see you. Give them our love." Then his aunt and uncle thanked them again and gave Wendell train fare. They shut the door.

"Do you have demon money to use?" Wendell asked Alana and the others.

"We can manage. I have to let my dad know our plans first."

Then they returned to the Hall of Records, walking together as before, keeping close so they didn't lose anyone. Once inside the Hall of Records, Alana updated her dad on the computer. She explained what they were going to do for Jared, and then she and the others, who would travel with her, would come to see him.

"See you when you get here then," her dad said.

Then they trudged through the deepening snow to the train station to buy their tickets.

"I wonder what part of Earth world they ended up in," Alana said, as they had their tickets in hand and waited for the westbound train to arrive.

"In this direction, maybe someplace in New Mexico. If we don't travel too far, maybe West Texas," Jared said, trying to calculate where a portal might deposit them. They just had to hope it was somewhere near a town.

The train pulled to a stop, and they climbed aboard and found the luxurious stateroom they had bought tickets for, got in, and shut the door. Gold brocade covered the seats, and they had three windows that looked onto the vista, two on the interior of the train, and one in the door. Except for the windows facing outside, the train had only a view of snow.

This wasn't half bad. Hunter closed the shades to the stateroom so no one would see Alana if any Matusa happened to walk past their room. They removed their parkas, hats, and gloves and stored them in overhead bins.

After a few minutes, the train zoomed off.

They watched out the window as the snowstorm didn't seem to be letting up.

"See anything further?" Alana asked Celeste.

She shook her head. "Sometimes I have one vision and no others concerning that incident. Sometimes I see more glimpses of the event, the same, and different."

They'd traveled in silence for about half an hour, Jared constantly checking his watch. Hunter wrapped his arm around Alana, and she rested her head against him. Wendell and Celeste watched the snow, while Samson observed Hunter and Alana.

Up until then, all they had heard was the clickety-clacking of the train traveling on the tracks. Then they heard a strange creaking and groaning.

Wendell stiffened. "I've ridden the trains all my life. I've never heard that sound before."

Celeste and Samson held onto their seats. Hunter tightened his hold on Alana as she and Jared grabbed the seats.

"Like…a train derailment?" Celeste asked, hurrying to pull on her jacket, gloves, and hat.

Everyone followed her lead. If they were thrown from the train, they needed to be bundled up, and it could offer them a little protection from the cold and the impact.

A huge crashing sound ahead of them reached them, grinding, metal screeching, crunching, train cars buckling, and flying off the tracks.

11

E verything was dark as Alana tried to figure out where she was. She'd lost hold of Hunter in the crash, but she was still in the train car. It was on its side now, and her left arm was throbbing with pain. She thought she might have broken it. She heard screaming and shrieks all up and down the tracks, people calling for their loved ones. She called out her friends' names, but no one responded.

The windows were gone and snow was filling them, which were now on the bottom of the stateroom. Looking up, she saw the aisle windows and door to their room where Hunter had closed the shades still shut. She pulled them open to see the room above theirs, but they had the shades pulled on their glass windows. She couldn't see any light up above.

She felt around in the room she was in, searching for any of her friends, and found a body, warm, lying in the snow, but not stirring and smelled Jared's scent. "Jared?"

Her head was pounding, and she wasn't thinking clearly. She used her magic to create light and saw that only Jared was with her. The others must have been thrown through the windows. "Jared, wake up."

She turned him over so his back was against the snow, and found a gash on the side of his head. She ran her hand over the wound, summoning her skills as a healer to heal him, but she was in so much pain, she was having a time concentrating.

Their demon healing would start to heal them much faster than humans, but she was sure her arm was broken, and she would need to set it before she could use her magic on it to heal it.

"Jared." She shook his shoulder. She was afraid the others would end up with hypothermia if they'd survived the train wreck, had been injured, and were out in the snow and cold.

People were still shouting and crying, but she didn't hear any of her friends' voices.

"Jared, you're safe here for the moment. I've got to look for the others." Alana hated to leave him without letting him know she was all right and would return for him. But she had to search for everyone else and bring them back there and heal them, if she could.

Working with only one good arm was going to be a trial though. She yanked open the door. Now she had to climb up into the room above her. What if their windows hadn't shattered? What if she couldn't get out that way? She might have to crawl through the hall until she found the exit.

She thought that would be easier than trying to climb above her head with only one good arm. Crawling with only one good arm was a feat too though. She kept blacking out and waking to find she'd made it a little further from their room. She hoped it wouldn't be long before she reached the end. It was amazing how long the passenger cars were when she was so injured. When she first climbed aboard, it didn't seem like it was any distance at all.

Someone was crying in a room above her, and she called out, "Can I help you?"

"Mommy hurt," a small girl said.

"Okay, I'm going to pull your door open. The train is resting on its side, so you need to stay away from the door, or you'll fall through."

"Mommy on the door."

Alana hesitated. She knew if she opened the door, she would have to catch the injured, or dead woman, and with only one good arm, that was going to be impossible. But if she was alive and Alana could heal her, she had to do it.

"All right. I'm injured too, so I'm going to open the door and try to catch your mommy. But you stay away from the door. I can't catch both of you at the same time. I'll try to heal her." It was too short a distance, so she knew she wouldn't have time to levitate her.

Alana took a deep breath, let it out, then pulled the door open. A female Elantus demon fell out, and Alana had to use both arms to catch her. Shrieking pain shot through Alana's broken arm, and she passed out.

"Mommy, Mommy, Mommy," a little girl said, peering through the open doorway as Alana opened her eyes and could focus. The girl's mother was lying across her, but she was warm and breathing. Alana worked hard to move her off her so she could check for injuries. She had a bad gash on her forehead too.

The little girl appeared uninjured.

"I'm going to try and heal her first. You stay there while I do that. Then I'll bring you down." She hoped the woman would be feeling well enough to bring her daughter down on her own, given Alana's injuries.

Alana worked on the woman for about ten minutes, and then she stirred. Her blue eyes stared up at Alana. "Kubiteron, healer. My daughter!"

"She's up there. I've broken my arm, and it needs to be set before I can heal it. Can you get her?"

The woman stood unsteadily and reached up for her daughter. She took her in her arms and hugged her tight.

"Is it just the two of you?" Alana asked, hoping they hadn't lost anyone.

"Yes."

"I'm leaving the train to look for my friends. I think they were thrown from the train. The windows were broken. My friend Jared, an Elantus demon also, is in the room at the bottom of the train, three rooms back. I didn't want to leave him alone, but, though I tried to heal him, he's still unconscious."

"Yes, yes, of course. I'm Emma."

"Alana."

"Thank you and good luck."

"Thank you." Alana continued on her way, while the woman and her daughter headed back to see Jared. She heard more commotion in some of the rooms, but she couldn't stop now. She had to find her friends and take care of them, and then she would see to any others who needed her healing abilities.

When she finally reached the steps, she realized she would have to climb up them to get out of the train. At this moment, she wished she could fly. Levitation!

HUNTER HAD HURRIED to dig through the snow for everyone he could find, sure his friends had to be somewhere near where he'd been thrown. Demons of all types were searching for their family or friends in the wreckage, some sporting injuries, cuts and abrasions, and worse. He'd sprained his wrist and injured his shoulder. But nothing was keeping him from looking for Alana and the rest of his friends.

Then he saw Wendell trying to dig himself out of the soft snow. That was the only good thing about all the snowfall they'd had. It was soft and powdery, or he was sure their injuries would have been much worse.

"Wendell," Hunter said, hurrying to join him and pull him out of the piled-up snow. "Are you okay?"

"Yeah. Where is everybody?" Wendell asked, looking around.

"You're the first one I've found."

"Alana?"

Hunter shook his head. It was killing him not knowing where she was, or if she was badly injured. He refused to believe she could be dead.

Someone grunted nearby, cursing.

"Samson?" Hunter hurried a few feet away to reach the Samuria.

"Where's Alana?" Samson sputtered, wiping the snow from his eyes.

"We haven't located her or the others yet. Are you all right?"

"Bruised, but nothing to write home about."

Wendell and Hunter gave him a hand up.

Wendell frowned at Hunter. "You're favoring your left arm."

"Sprained wrist. No big deal."

"Alana can heal it when we find her," Samson said, but they were already digging around in the snow for anyone else.

They moved closer to the wreckage when they couldn't find anyone who might have been thrown from the train. "In her vision, Celeste said she'd been pinned under the wreckage," Hunter said, and they tried to find where their room had been and checked the area around it. He prayed she wasn't completely covered by the wreckage or they would never find her.

Then Hunter saw a gloved hand sticking out of the snow. "Over here!"

Everyone hurried to join him and started pulling the snow away from the buried figure. It was Celeste, and she was unconscious.

"Celeste," Hunter said, reaching down to listen to see if she had a heartbeat. It was faint, but she had one. "We have to lift the train off her."

"No way. It's too heavy," Wendell said.

Samson said, "Alana, she can use her power of levitation."

"I'm not sure she could lift anything this heavy. We have to find her and Jared though," Hunter said, sick with worry. "Samson, stay with Celeste. If she comes to, let her know we're getting her out of there soon. We haven't found Alana and Jared yet. And, Samson, if you start to lose her, give her CPR, okay?"

Samson nodded. He was so studious and loved learning everything he could, Hunter figured he had read up on it while he'd stayed in their world.

Wendell hurried off with Hunter, both of them seeing other demons in need. But he had to find Alana and Jared first.

Hunter grabbed hold of a couple of railings on the top of the train, that were now on the side and lifted himself up until he was on top where the opening was. And saw Alana sprawled out on the floor, dead to the world down below.

"Alana!" Hunter's heart was practically jumping out of his chest as he hurried to climb into the train to reach her.

Looking worried, Wendell was peering down at them. "Is she okay?"

"Oh." Alana's eyes fluttered open as Hunter gathered her in his arms.

"Alana."

"Ow, ow, watch the arm. It's broken."

"Sorry. Jared?"

"He's unconscious in the room we were in. A woman with her little girl is with him. I healed him the best I could." She looked up to see Wendell. "Celeste? Samson?"

"Samson's with Celeste. She's pinned beneath the train, like she foretold. Do you think you could levitate it?"

"And heal Hunter's wrist," Wendell said.

"I'm not sure I can levitate anything that heavy. I can heal your wrist, and maybe the three of you guys can lift the train?"

"Yeah." Hunter pulled off his glove, wincing, then frowned. "You sure you can do it? It won't take too much out of you."

She gave him a scowly look. "If I had to beat on your chest, that might do it."

He smiled at her, loving her. "Nothing quite that drastic this time."

She ran her hand over his wrist, silently chanting a spell, and within seconds, his wrist felt back to normal. He rubbed it, glad she was able to heal it. She was a godsend to him.

"Did she fix it?" Wendell asked.

"Yeah." Hunter pulled his glove back on, then helped her to stand. "Okay, so you can't heal your arm?"

"No. It's broken and needs to be set first. Are you sure you don't have any other injuries? You're still wincing."

"My shoulder, but—"

"Which one?"

"Right."

She healed it for him and shook her head. "Anywhere else?"

"That's it. Thanks, Alana. We need to mobilize Your arm first. Stay here." Hunter opened one of the doors to a room and found a semi-conscious male Camaran demon inside, but he had a bag, and Hunter thought he could make a brace with that. "Hey, how badly are you injured?" he asked the man.

"Just...just came to. What...what happened?"

"Train derailment. A Kubiteron is with me. She can try to heal you, but she has a broken arm. I need to brace it so she doesn't move it. Can I use your bag?"

He smiled.

Hunter thought he was delirious. "Sir, she can heal people. We have a friend trapped under the train. She can help her. But before that, I need to immobilize Alana's broken arm."

"I'm...a physician."

"Oh. Here, let me help you out of there, and we can crawl up to the exit where she's waiting for me."

"Crawl?"

"The car is on its side."

The physician nodded. He was still really out of it.

Hunter climbed into the room and then tossed the doctor's bag out of the room. He helped lift the doctor out, then climbed out after him. "To your left, that way."

The doctor was in front of him and moved so slowly, Hunter wished he'd been ahead of him so he could have reached Alana sooner.

"Why aren't rescue workers out here helping everyone?" Hunter asked.

"Holiday and the sudden winter storm will make it difficult to reach us. If I had to guess, I would say we are in the mountains."

Oh, great, so even after they saved themselves, those that they could, they might have to wait hours to be rescued from there? And then what? Taken back to where they'd been? Or go forward to where they were going?

12

W hen the doctor finally reached Alana, he told her he was a physician and took a look at her arm. "I'm going to straighten it, but it's bound to hurt."

She nodded.

Then he straightened it, and the color drained from her already pale cheeks.

Together the doctor and Hunter created a brace and sling out of his bag for her.

"Thanks, Doctor," she said, "and Hunter."

"Hey, Doc Clyne!" Wendell shouted from up above.

The doctor looked up, then smiled broadly. "You're back!"

"Yeah, because of them, and some of their other friends."

The doctor eyed Hunter and Alana with suspicion.

"Half human," Hunter explained.

"Gate guardian," Alana added.

"Thanks to both of you," the doctor said. "Wendell's my favorite nephew."

Alana ran her hand over her arm to help heal it. "It'll take longer to mend because torn ligaments and broken bones always do, but it feels much better. Thanks."

Then the doctor made his way out of the train with Wendell's help, carrying the contents of his medical bag with him.

Hunter helped Alana out of the train, and though he thought the doctor would take a look at other demons who needed his assistance, he trudged through the snow to see to Celeste too.

"What had you hoped to do?" the doctor asked, looking as though he thought she was a lost cause.

"Levitate the car. I might not be able to manage, but I'll try. I passed out when I tried to levitate myself out of the train, but that was because my arm was hurting so badly. And someone needs to pull Celeste out. If that doesn't work, maybe some of you can lift the car while I try levitating it and someone pulls her out."

The doctor was staring at Alana, slack-jawed.

"Half-witch. Is everyone ready?" Alana said.

"Just a second. Doctor, can you pull Celeste out? The rest of us guys will try to lift the car while Alana tries to levitate it. Alana, let us know if it's not going to work," Hunter said.

"You'll know if I can't do it."

The doctor took hold of Celeste's shoulders. "Ready."

Samson and Wendell were on one side of her, holding the edge of the train. Hunter stood on the other side. He swore Wendell was still afraid of him.

Then Alana held up her good arm, and furrowed her brow, trying to concentrate.

Hunter heard the car groan a little, and he felt it lift slightly. "Pull," he shouted to the doctor. Even if they had to inch Celeste out, that was better than nothing.

He knew Alana was struggling to levitate the heavy car, and the guys were all trying to lift it, but it seemed they weren't making any progress. The doctor was straining to pull Celeste out when suddenly a couple more men joined them. One helped with Celeste. The other helped Hunter.

He knew his scent right away. Bentos. His father.

"You always seem to be in a bind, but you never call on me. Why is that?" Bentos asked.

"Seems you are in the same mess we're in."

"Alana's uncle said she was on the train heading to East End. I happened to be at the Hall of Records, checking on him."

"Checking on Alana, you mean."

"We've got her!" the doctor and other man shouted.

Alana said, "Release your hold on the car!"

Everyone scrambled away, and she dropped it. Then she sat down hard on the snow. Hunter joined her and wrapped his arm around her.

"Celeste," she whispered.

"You can look after her as soon as you have your wind back. The doctor is seeing to her."

Alana squeezed Hunter's hand. "Check on Jared."

He kissed her cheek. "You'll be all right?"

"Yes, but I worry about him and Celeste."

"I'll see to Jared." Hunter glanced at Samson, hating to ask, but Samson immediately moved over to watch over Alana. "Don't get any ideas," Hunter said to his dad.

He shrugged. "Pappalios said you have your rings already. I'm too late." He gave him an evil smile.

Hunter just had to make sure his dad didn't see that they weren't wearing the rings yet.

Wendell was eyeing Bentos with suspicion, but he moved over to help his uncle with Celeste.

Hunter trudged through the snow and climbed onto the train again, crawling through to their room. The door was open, and a woman was sleeping with her daughter, her arm around Jared too, as if he were family.

"Jared!" Hunter said, climbing down into the room. The woman and her daughter screamed.

Jared opened his eyes. He looked groggy, but hell, he was glad to see his friend was conscious.

"I have the worst headache. What happened?"

The woman and her daughter looked so terrified, Hunter said, "Tell them I'm half human and your best friend, and my girlfriend saved them."

The woman didn't look reassured.

"What Hunter said. Where is everyone?"

"Train wreck. Celeste was pinned beneath the car. We got her out, and Wendell's uncle is a doctor, and he's seeing to her. But I had to learn if you were all right."

"Yeah, yeah." Jared started to stand but clutched his ribs.

"Broken? Bruised?"

"They hurt like hell."

"Okay, as long as you're okay, I mean, you're going to live, I'll leave you here. We'll bring Celeste inside out of the cold as soon as we can move her. You take care of the lady and little one in the meantime."

"All right. What...what about everyone else?"

"Samson's fine. Alana wants to heal everyone she can, but she has a broken arm." Hunter explained all the rest.

"Okay." Jared sank down next to the woman and her child. They were all shivering.

"Do have some more clothes?" Hunter asked the woman.

"Yeah. Four rooms down, and up above."

"All right, I'll get your things and toss them down." As soon as Hunter climbed out of the room and found her statement room, he grabbed a kid's bag, a couple of blankets, pillows, winter jackets, gloves, hats, and her bag. He began moving the items and then dropping them down into their room.

The woman dressed her daughter warmly first, and then herself. She wrapped the blankets around her and her daughter and Jared. "Thank you."

"You're welcome. Did Alana see to your ribs, Jared?" Hunter asked.

"She probably didn't know they were injured."

"Okay, it's too difficult for her to climb in and out of the car, so she'll take care of it as soon as she can."

"No worries. Take care of Celeste."

"Will do."

The woman took one of the blankets and offered it to Hunter. "For Celeste."

He smiled. "Thank you." He didn't mind other demons fearing him for what he was, but when he needed to help them, he wanted them to realize that was his only intention.

Then he made his way back outside with the blanket. Alana was hunched over Celeste, casting one of her healing chants. Samson was with her, but Wendell, the doctor, and Bentos were gone.

"Has she come to?" Hunter asked, covering Celeste with the blanket.

Alana let out her breath and stopped the chant. "No, but we don't want her to. Both her legs are broken, the doctor said. He set them, but we have nothing to use to keep them immobile."

"Where's my dad?"

"Barking orders over that way. He's making people look for supplies, including something we can use for Celeste. Everyone has to grab their warm clothes and get dressed, but many are in shock and so cold, they're not thinking straight. They weren't like us, and knew to dress warmly before the train wreck happened."

"If you don't need me here, I'll help find clothes and something for Celeste," Samson said.

"Yeah, thanks, Samson," Hunter said, appreciating that he looked after Alana for him. Even if Samson thought it was his duty. "Jared's ribs are broken or bruised."

"Great," Alana said.

"He said to just take care of Celeste."

"He's okay, then?" Alana asked.

"Yeah, he's staying with the woman and her daughter. He can't climb out, and it's too difficult for you to climb back in. We'll need to move everyone back into the train for protection until a rescue effort is underway."

"I would think they would be here by now." She motioned with her good hand toward the mountains. "Until I saw how difficult the terrain is. We're just lucky it derailed before it crossed that chasm. That's what Wendell said. He has traveled this way a few times to see his Uncle Clyne."

"Did it derail before we reached the chasm?"

She peered in that direction. "I don't know. We can't see anything for the snow. Do you want to check it out?"

"Yeah, I do, but I'm not leaving you alone, in case either you or Celeste need me."

They waited. Though he wanted to do something, anything. Still, he didn't want to leave her alone either.

She finally put her hand on his arm. "Go, help the others."

"But..."

She tugged at his hand. "I'm fine. I don't need your protection. But everyone needs your help."

He leaned down and kissed her. "I won't be too far away." Then he headed to where his father was issuing orders. "Dad, did you find something to bind Celeste's wounds."

"Yeah, check over there."

Hunter grabbed the gear and hurried back to Alana and Celeste. When he reached them, he said, "My dad neglected to tell me they'd gathered something already that would work."

"He's helping, though, right?"

"Yeah. They've gathered a lot of items. Everyone's being looked after." Hunter began to work on Celeste's right leg.

"I wish I could help you bind her legs." Alana began to numb them so they didn't hurt so much.

"You did just what needed to be done." He finished binding Celeste's legs.

Celeste groaned.

"Celeste, are you okay?" Alana asked, taking her hand.

"Cold. My legs..."

"Uhm, they're..."

"Just say it. I'm a demon."

"Broken. But the doctor said he thinks that's all there is to it. I mean, not that that's not bad, but nothing's crushed. And that's what he was worried about. We need to get you inside the train so you'll be warmer," Alana said.

"As long as the train isn't moving. How long has it been?"

"A couple of hours."

Celeste frowned. "And nobody's come for us?"

"We're in the mountains."

Celeste glanced around and groaned. "Great. I guess we didn't do what we should have to prevent this from happening."

Alana shook her head. "The train stopped before we went off a bridge."

"Oh, that would have hurt."

"After we get Celeste inside, I want to see what's ahead. Depending on how far we are from East End, maybe we could walk out of here," Hunter said.

"We could return to Earth world." Alana had been thinking about it as an option.

"It would depend on where we would end up. And Jared had his heart set on learning where his parents are."

"Like that's happening any time soon," Alana said.

Hunter lifted Celeste in his arms. "Come. We'll see if there's a way to get you down to Jared so you can heal his ribs."

Several of the demons helped them to lift Celeste onto the train.

Then Hunter and Samson helped Alana inside. She finally reached their room and peered down below. "Jared, I've come to help you."

Hunter was waiting for her and took hold of her as carefully as he could, Jared reaching up for her. He grabbed hold of her, and they both groaned. Then she began to work on Jared's ribs. "I need you healed so you can help everyone else."

"I need to also," the Elantus mother said.

"You need to stay with your daughter."

Samson peered down at them. "Everyone's inside now, so they can stay as warm as possible. There was another healer and he and the doctor were taking care of the injured. Bentos is ready to kill whoever hasn't come to rescue us. I'm sorry about not getting the supplies for Celeste's legs, but I was forced to help carry the injured inside."

"It was done," Celeste said. "No worries."

"If you'll be all right," Hunter said to Alana, "I'm going to check out the bridge."

"I'm coming with you," Jared said. "I feel fine, thanks to you, Alana. Thank you for being on the team."

"Thank you for all your gadgets."

"I'll stay with Alana," Samson said.

Then Jared and Hunter left the train. The snow was letting up.

"Where are you going?" Bentos asked.

"To see what became of the rest of the train," Hunter said.

Bentos joined them. "And to see if the bridge is still there. Why don't you take us to Earth world."

"You would like that, wouldn't you?" Hunter asked. His dad was always devious.

"It was only an idea."

"Alana already suggested it. But I say no. There might be some dangerous demons on the train who would cause humans real trouble."

"You mean like me?" Bentos laughed.

"Tell me about my brother."

"Half-brother. He's not ready to know what he is."

"I knew before this! And I had to deal with it on my own! Do you want him to have to do the same thing? Wait, you think...you think he'll be like me if I speak with him. And you want him to be loyal to you so that he lets you into Earth world whenever you want to."

"His mother does that."

Hunter still didn't trust his father's motives.

Then they saw the bridge, some of it had collapsed, and a train car was hanging off the edge.

"Don't tell me you want to save anyone in that passenger car," Bentos said. "You are hurting our kind's reputation. The lesser demons will no longer fear us if you become their...hero."

"That's what I do, Dad."

Bentos smiled at him.

Hunter scowled. He rarely called him dad. He didn't know what came over him to do so now. Maybe because, when push came to shove, he had helped the rest of the demons in their time of need.

"Jared, are you coming?"

"Uh, yeah, you know I am. I wish now that Alana was with us."

Hunter began making his way across the train bridge that was still intact. "To do what?"

"What if she could levitate people out of the car?"

"She has been injured."

"Yeah, but still..."

"I could go back and get her," Bentos said.

"No."

"I will," Jared said. "I'll be back soon. Don't go rescuing everyone before I get back with her." Then Jared ran through the snow as fast as he could.

Hunter wasn't waiting. He inched toward the car. The cables were holding it, but the car was swaying in the wind.

"This is foolhardy." Bentos followed him along the bridge.

Hunter shouted, "Is anyone alive down there?"

There was no response.

"Don't you dare climb down there to find out," Bentos ordered.

Hunter shouted again, "We've come to save you! Is there anyone alive there?"

"Yes!" Came a chorus of shouts.

Hunter was glad, but he knew this was risky business. "I'm coming." If nothing else, if the car began to fall, he would pull everyone he could through a portal in Earth world and hope that they landed somewhere safely.

"You cannot be my son," Bentos said, waiting at the cable, watching to see that Hunter made it to the car.

"No, I'm too heroic."

Hunter kept climbing down until he could reach the opening, and slid in to the aisle, grabbing a door handle to stop himself from falling all the way to the end of the car.

Demons began opening doors to their rooms, then looked shocked to see a Matusa coming for them.

"I'm here to rescue you," Hunter said.

13

H unter couldn't believe how many passengers were on the train. "I want to help those who are uninjured first. We'll have to figure out a way to get everyone else out safely."

He was surprised to see a Matusa making his way past the other demons, who were hanging onto parts of the train to keep from falling.

"I go first," the Matusa said to Hunter as if they were part of a Matusa brotherhood.

"Be my guest." Hunter motioned to the way he'd climbed in. He had no intention of helping an able-bodied Matusa who could do what Hunter did on his own. He should have already left the train. Hunter figured he hadn't thought he could manage, or that someone would come to their rescue before long. Fat chance of that.

"I thought you had come to rescue us!" the Matusa said.

"Yes, for everyone who *needs* rescuing."

"Take my baby, please," a woman begged Hunter and handed the baby in some kind of body bag to a man holding onto the doorjamb ahead of her.

He passed the baby along until Hunter had ahold of him. "How many children are onboard?" Hunter asked, trying to keep from falling, and fastening the baby around his shoulders and waist, while another man held onto Hunter with his free hand.

A head count was made.

"Seven, including the lady's baby," a man called out. He looked like he was wearing the uniform of a train conductor.

"How many of those can fit into a carrier like this?" Hunter figured he could return with the carrier, once the baby was safe up above, and carry more babies out. If there were more.

"Three of them," a woman said. "But you can only take one at a time."

"All right. I'll be back for the other two after I give the baby to another passenger waiting above for me." Hunter knew his dad would love to hear that. Just as much as the mother would love to hear Hunter was handing her baby over to another Matusa.

Ensuring the baby was properly secured, he began the climb up, the whole time the train was creaking and groaning. He didn't like the sound of it. He hoped that if they could take some of the weight out of the car, the strain on the cable wouldn't be so great. But the wind through the chasm was pushing the car also, making it sway.

Once he made it to the top, he climbed up the cable, and Bentos helped him onto the bridge.

"This is it? One baby?" Bentos asked incredulously.

"I'm bringing up the children first." Hunter took the baby out of the carrier and handed him to his father.

"What do you want me to do with it?"

"Take care of him until I bring up the mother." Then Hunter climbed down the cable. He sure was going to get a workout today and this was supposed to be spring break for him too.

He'd entered the car when he heard Alana yell, "Hunter!"

He knew she would want to kill him for not waiting for her, but what if the train crashed before she'd arrived?

Someone had already passed the second baby up to the first cabin, and Hunter didn't have as far to climb down into the car. That was much better. He needed his strength to make it up the cable each time. He secured the second baby and made his way back up to the cable. He wasn't sure how many trips he could make before he was totally worn out. Then again, as a Matusa, he was the strongest of the demons.

When he reached for the cable, Alana was standing on the train bridge, scowling at him, holding her arm in the sling.

Bentos was standing beside her. No baby.

"What did you do with the baby?" Hunter growled.

Bentos helped him to the bridge. "Jared's got the baby. Or...at least he had."

A grandmotherly type was standing on the snowbank with the baby wrapped in her arms.

Jared crossed the bridge to take the second baby in his arms. Even removing the baby from the carrier was dangerous as they all balanced on the bridge. But Hunter had to admit he felt a lot more respect for his dad as he held onto Hunter so he wouldn't fall while he pulled the baby free of the carrier. He passed her to Alana, and she handed her off to Jared, who carefully made his way back across the bridge to another waiting woman.

"What do you want me to do? I can't climb down there," Alana said.

"I'll bring the people up, one by one, and you can levitate them over to the land. If they can manage the bridge, you could set them down on it. But they may be in shock, or too terrified to navigate it."

"All right."

"I'll carry the children up first, and then we'll work on the adults together."

Before Hunter could climb back down the cable, the Matusa finally chanced climbing up on his own.

Bentos laughed. "You've been down there all this time and finally got the courage to try it on your own, Viton?"

The Matusa's eyes widened when he saw Alana. So did Alana's.

"If you ever think of grabbing me again, I'll—" she said.

"I'll take care of you," Hunter warned the Matusa. "I'm her mate."

"And Hunter is my son, so you don't want to aggravate me," Bentos said.

Viton looked at Alana and said, "You could have done so much better." He gave her an evil smirk, then made it across the bridge.

Hunter gave him a dark look, then headed back down the cable.

Someone had made a makeshift harness for a four-year-old that would work for a couple more young ones, a man told him. After taking the last baby up, Hunter began carrying up the next older children. Hunter strapped on the next child and began the climb again.

After carrying the last of the small children up, the last two kids were twelve-year-old twins. Hunter said, "My mate is going to levitate the adults over to the land mass unless any are fine with crossing the train bridge. It's covered in snow and a little slippery. You'll have to watch your step. After taking the twins, I want to take the moms of all the children."

"She can levitate us," the one girl said.

"Yeah, sure." Then she frowned. "What kind of demon does that?"

"My demon. All right, girls, one at a time. Then the moms." Hunter helped the first girl up to the cable, and once she was there, Hunter said to Alana, "She wants you to levitate her."

"Over there. I don't trust the bridge," the young girl said.

"You got it." Alana called on her ability to levitate the girl over to the snowbank where several of the other passengers had gathered to help anyone from this car. Then she did the same for her sister.

Afterward, Alana levitated each of the moms. They were so happy to be reunited with their children.

Hunter felt good about that. That was his mission in life: take care of demons and return them to their own world, but taking care of them here worked too.

Alana managed to levitate fourteen more adults. All that was left behind now was the injured and family and friends who wouldn't leave them behind until they were taken care of first. And the train conductor. Hunter wished he could bring Alana down here to see if she could use her healing magic on them.

With her broken arm in a sling, she wouldn't be able to manage the climb down, or to be able to hold on, if she could manage to levitate herself into the car. Not when it was standing on end and swinging in the wind.

One female Matusa with a broken hip didn't have anyone to help her so Hunter took her first. "Viton, that snake, left me behind at the first chance he had. I can't believe he could have left before this and had to wait to see you manage first with a couple of babies. I will kill Viton for leaving me behind when I'm feeling better," she promised.

The train conductor wouldn't leave until the last of the passengers had been helped out. Some of the men had climbed out on their own. Some couldn't make it up the cable and Alana assisted those.

The train conductor suffered from a dislocated shoulder. Hunter and the man braced themselves until Hunter could put it back in place for him. "Alana will help heal it when we reach the safe place."

"She sounds like a real wonder," the conductor said, slowly making his way to the top, groaning with pain.

"She is." And all Hunter's. "How many cars were in front of this one?"

"The three engines all made it before the bridge collapsed. Another passenger car fell into the ravine. It's sitting right-side up on the ground. I've shouted to see if there are any survivors, but no response. We were afraid our car would join them and end up crushing them. Rescue operations will have to send mountain climbers down to see if there are any survivors."

Or maybe Alana could levitate Hunter down there to check for survivors. He didn't want to leave anyone behind if they didn't have to.

"You want me to do what?" Alana asked Hunter.

"Listen, what if the car that's hanging by a cable breaks away and lands on top of the other one down below? What if people are trapped in there, injured, in shock, with no way to get help? Maybe not for hours? They could end up perishing. If you could levitate me down there, I could see if anyone's alive who still needs rescuing. We still have no idea when anyone is coming for us." Hunter wrapped his arms around her and hugged her close. "Let's do this."

"What if I drop you?"

"You won't. But if you did, I would come back and snuggle next to you, just like Indigo does. You'll never get rid of me."

"Oh, that would be just great. I would be in a constant freezer zone. Okay, all right. Let's do this."

He kissed her mouth. "Okay, send me down."

"If you're going for the Hero of the Demon World award, I believe you've already earned it."

"Not me."

Alana levitated Hunter and began to move him slowly down to the snowy ground next to the train car. She wanted him to hurry.

The car swinging from the train tracks sounded worse by the minute.

Hunter shouted out, "Any survivors?"

She heard cheers from inside the car, and people who were able to begin climbing out to greet him. Until they saw he was a Matusa. Poor Dark One. He pointed to Alana, she waved and smiled, and he explained what she was going to do.

People on the land mass by the bridge cheered the people down below, and it was heartwarming to see the comradery.

"How many of them are there?" she hollered to the conductor.

"Forty-two," he said.

"Hunter, I'll take two at a time. We'll never get this done before dark."

"Are you sure?"

"Yeah. If I don't, I won't make it. I can do more, if it's a couple of adults and a child."

While she was transporting small groups of people, Hunter and other uninjured passengers were carrying out the dead and injured and getting them ready to transport.

She was ready to collapse, she was so tired. Hunter was the last one to be lifted, but he hollered, "Wait just a second!" Then he dashed back into the train.

"Hurry, Hunter. This cable is fraying up here!"

Then she heard it snapping. "Hunter!"

He dashed back outside. "Okay, do it!"

She began to levitate him, moving him toward the canyon wall where the rest of the people were waiting for him in anticipation.

The cable snapped to the car where she was standing, shaking the bridge. She lost her footing on the slippery bridge and fell off it. Breaking her concentration on the levitation spell, she was horrified when Hunter fell also. In freefall, she quickly levitated the two of them at different points, not having thought she could do that, but her witch's skills were improving, the more she practiced them. Something her Uncle Stephen always reminded her.

She pulled Hunter up to where she was waiting mid-air for him, then went to hug him before she levitated them the rest of the way to the secure area. But something was meowing inside his parka, and she frowned down at it.

"Stowaway kitten," he said, smiling at her.

"You are so…human."

He smiled again. "Hurry and get us to the top of the cliff. The kitten has claws that could rival a Matusa's."

She laughed. "I will remember this always."

"About saving all the people, with your help. It was the only way we could have done this."

"About rescuing the kitten at the last." She noticed a woman taking pictures of them and wondered how long she'd been taking them.

The doctor and another healer had taken care of the injured as much as they could. And everyone shared what they could with each other, while Hunter gave the kitten to the twin girls to take care of.

Hunter was going to give such a bad name for their kind, Alana was thinking, smiling at him. He sure could be cute. Alana thought maybe she could help everyone move two of the cars right-side up to make it easier to stay in them until they were rescued.

"Hey, if we could do it, we would have a lot more comfortable quarters, and it would make it easier to move in and out of the cars if they were right-side up," she said.

With the men and older boys, and a few hardy women helping, and Alana's levitation spell, they managed to right two of them. A third was on its top and it would have been impossible for her to flip around. Though maybe someday, if she needed such an ability, she could. But even with these two cars, she'd had a lot of muscle to help move them.

"Your Dad's steaks sure sound good about now," Hunter said, snuggling with Alana in their cabin, a blanket over the broken windows as he and his friends accommodated the Elantus woman and her child. Her room was being used by some of the people who'd been in the cars they'd lost in the ravine.

Jared sighed. "You know what, I'm ready for the steak too. We can go to East End some other time to learn where a portal would lead. After we've well-recuperated. Besides, if I find my parents, then what? I would need one of you to help get them back."

Samson agreed. "We work well as a team. We should stick together."

Celeste nodded. "Well, I mean, I'm not going anywhere until I can walk again."

Wendell sat next to Celeste. "Do you want to rest your head on my lap?" She was stretched out on one of the seats to accommodate her broken legs. Samson and Jared were sitting on the floor. The Elantus woman and her daughter shared the seat with Alana and Hunter.

"Yeah, thanks."

Hunter wondered if Wendell liked Celeste because she'd saved him, and she was a Camaran demon like him. But Samson watched them warily, looking as though he wished he'd offered first.

They all napped as much as they could in the cramped quarters. Four hours later, they heard shouts from the other train car behind them.

That's when they heard a train pulling up on the tracks above them where their cars had once sat.

Hunter was on his feet in an instant, ready to warn the train that the bridge was out, but it pulled to a stop.

Everyone who could climbed out of their cars, and medical staff and police officers were on hand, helping load the injured first, and then allowing everyone else to load into the remaining cars.

The journey back to West Station was quick while police officers took everyone's statements. Hunter was irritated when his friends wouldn't let him get a word in edgewise.

"You should have seen the two of them. Between Alana's ability to levitate the passengers from the two cars, and Hunter's aiding all of them to navigate the cars, the two of them saved many lives. You should have seen when the one car crashed into the other," Jared said. "It looked like a tin can crushed under the weight of someone's boot."

"And he saved a kitten," Alana said.

The policeman smiled but then lost the smile when he looked at Hunter's dark expression.

It was an inborn trait for a Matusa. He couldn't help himself. He was to be feared by lesser demons. Not made fun of, though he loved Alana for loving him for rescuing the kitten. And he was glad the girls cherished the fur ball. Though he hoped they had wanted him and didn't feel they had to take him because a Matusa gave it to them to care for. After their traumatic experience, he'd hoped the kitten would have helped take their mind off the experience.

"Bentos was ordering everyone about too, organizing people to assist others. That's Hunter's dad. Everybody that could, worked hard to help," Samson said.

"Yeah, my Uncle Clyne, the doctor? He was instrumental in aiding a lot of the injured. So was Alana and another healer," Jared said.

The policeman finally glanced at Hunter as if he should have asked him for his input first. "I have nothing to add. They said more than enough."

The Elantus woman spoke up. "Alana saved me when here she was concerned about her mate and her friends. She heard my girl crying and even though Alana had a broken arm, she still suffered, just to help me down from my room. The car was flipped on its side. I was unconscious. She healed me and brought me to stay with her injured friend while she went to help others."

"Thank you," the police officer said, turning to Alana to see if she had anything else to offer.

She shook her head.

"She levitated the two train cars so that they were upright, and we could rest more comfortably until help arrived," Jared added.

"Yeah, but without you and everyone else helping, I couldn't have done it by myself."

"Not me," Celeste said. "I haven't been able to help anyone do anything."

"You shared all kinds of fun stories with my daughter," the girl's mother said.

Celeste smiled.

The police officer again thanked them, and then he moved on to the next car.

Someone else came along with a camera and took pictures of them.

"Really?" Alana said.

He just winked, got their names, and hurried on his way.

"News reporter," Wendell said. "Cameron Parks. One of our biggest news announcers. I'm sure this is going to make some headline news. My parents are going to wonder what in the world I was doing traveling in the wrong direction."

"You were becoming a hero," Hunter said.

14

As soon as the train reached West Station, Hunter was relieved. Could they get free train transportation to Alana's dad's place? If they even wanted to ride the train.

They began to offload, Samson and Hunter carrying Celeste out of the train while Alana, Jared, and Wendell followed behind.

"Hey, that's the mayor," Wendell said. "News reporters, more police officers, hospital emergency staff, wow, what a circus."

Bentos met up with them and said, "I've got a van for us."

"Us?" Hunter wondered what his dad was up to.

"Yeah, us. I spoke to the mayor about you being heroes, and he arranged for a van to take us to East End."

"Wait, I see my dad!" Alana raced off to meet up with her dad. "Dad!"

"Alana!"

Hunter glanced at Jared.

"I'm going, I'm going." Jared raced after her to provide her protection.

"Well, maybe some of you want to ride in the van with me? Pappalios has invited me to dinner to celebrate your mating," Bentos said to Hunter.

"I'm riding with Alana and her dad," Hunter said.

"A van sounds good to me," Celeste said.

"I'll go with Celeste," Wendell said.

"Me too," Samson said, looking as though he was still supposed to protect Celeste as well as Alana now.

"Good. I'll lead the way."

"Why were you headed in the opposite direction on the train?" Hunter asked.

"I had planned to go home and change clothes. That sort of went out the window when we ended up in a train crash, now we're back here, and it's time for dinner."

After Hunter left Celeste in Samson and Wendell's care and joined Jared and Alana to ride with her father, he was surprised to hear where the conversation was going.

"You could have asked me where a portal would open from Seplichus to Earth world. It's Amarillo. When you return to Dallas, you can take a flight or a car ride, to the city."

"Why didn't you tell us you could come and pick us up?" Alana asked.

"You said you were going to East End first. Besides, I don't have a vehicle. I had to borrow this from a friend, and I usually only do so in emergencies. This was definitely an emergency," her dad said.

They soon arrived at her dad's place, and it was a veritable mansion. Nothing like the condo where her mother and she lived. "You live here all by yourself?"

"It was my family's estate. They're gone now. Passed away, so yes, I live here alone. Though I've brought your mother here whenever I can."

"On those secret trips she has made," Alana said.

"Yes."

"Wow," Jared said, "I thought we would be sleeping in sleeping bags on the living room floor."

"No, that's why I said everyone was welcome. We have room for everyone."

Bentos pulled up in the van behind them.

Before they could carry Celeste into the house, a couple of men wheeled a stretcher to the van.

"Oh, great. The royal treatment," Celeste said.

"I have a clinic of sorts here. Those of us who are gate guardians bring injured demons here to obtain medical treatment that we couldn't offer through our healers. I've already seen the reports on the news about Alana's broken arm and Celeste's broken legs. We'll have them x-rayed, and reset, if need be. Then, reduce the swelling, if necessary, and put you both in casts."

"Thanks, Dad."

"Thanks, Pappalios," Celeste added.

"I guess that means dinner will be delayed," Bentos said.

Everyone looked at him like he'd better not be annoyed about it.

He gave them a dark smile, and Hunter realized he was joking.

Everyone peeled out of their winter wear once they were inside, and a man took their cold-weather gear and put it in a coat room.

"I'm visiting you lots," Alana said.

"This summer for two months, right?" her dad said.

"Yeah."

"And me." Hunter had thought he would be demon hunting, but he couldn't leave Alana here for that long without seeing her.

"Absolutely," Pappalios said. He motioned to a large living area filled with couches and a wide-screen TV. "Make yourself at home, while we take care of the injured."

Bentos went for the controller.

Hunter stayed with Alana and Celeste. "Do you make a lot of money as a gate guardian?" Hunter asked her dad.

"Yes. People pay me to locate family members who have been taken into a portal from the surrounding area. I would like to say what I do is purely magnanimous, but as humans are fond of saying, we have to pay the bills."

Alana, Hunter, and her dad watched through a viewing window as Celeste was being x-rayed.

"But you don't rescue *everyone*," Hunter said.

"We can't. It takes time to pinpoint where they've gone, even after I've located where the portal had opened in our world. Once I've done that, it may take me some time, months or years even, to locate where the individual has gone. Or individuals, as the case may be."

"What about Jared's parents?" Alana asked.

"Nobody hired me to check into it. A gate guardian might not have been living in his region at the time, but I would think Jared's uncle would know something about that."

"We didn't know how all of this worked from your side," Alana said.

"Yeah, but his uncle said nothing about it." Which Hunter thought was odd. "Jared just turned nineteen." Which reminded Hunter that he needed to do something about celebrating it.

"When did this happen?" Alana asked, sounding annoyed with him.

"Sorry. We should have celebrated it. Two days ago. We were saving demons about that time, and it slipped my mind."

"We'll have a special celebration here," Pappalios said.

"Okay, so what would the situation have been, let's say twenty years ago? Jared's uncle said Jared hadn't been born yet when his parents were taken," Hunter said.

"Mortimer was there at one time. He might have already died before then. We don't have gate guardians for all regions. There are not enough of us to go around. So you have been a godsend in Earth world."

Alana frowned. "But I don't get paid. I'm still in school, but if I was paid for everyone I"—she cast a glance at Hunter and took hold of his hand—"we rescued, we could earn a living and still do a good deed. Otherwise, we're all going to have to go to work somewhere. We won't always have time to do this. Not if we need to support ourselves."

"I'll have my financial manager handle it. He'll have to coordinate with the regent ruler to let him know what you're doing in Earth world and that the people who have been returned, need their families to pay for your assistance. It might seem unfair that the summoners have done this, but, as long as the demons can be returned unharmed to this world, anyone involved in the work should be paid."

"Thanks."

"You can't expect to do this without earning a living at it. All gate guardians are paid. Yours is an exceptional case because you rescue them without anyone asking you to do so. But they want to return, so it's not like you're forcing this on them. They're forced to go to Earth world."

"What about if the family can't afford to pay for them?" Alana asked.

"The state has a fund for cases like that. The regent rulers don't expect us to work for free."

She smiled. "Yes! I thought I was going to be stuck ghostbusting with my mom."

"I don't think you'll have to worry about it. Not after everyone sees the news about what you did today."

An x-ray technician wheeled Celeste out of the room, and Celeste smiled at them. "Good news. They don't have to rebreak the bones. Jared's uncle was able to set them perfectly, and you helped them to begin to heal," she said to Alana. "I'm off to the cast room. I'm glad, but this puts a damper on my surfing plans."

"That is good news." Alana looked hopeful hers would be just as good as she walked into the x-ray room to have her arm scanned.

Hunter was quiet then, watching Alana.

"You make a great team. I couldn't be happier for the both of you," Pappalios said and handed Hunter two gold rings, both etched with strange symbols. "Wear them in good health."

Hunter smiled. "Thanks."

"And, don't tell Alana I said so, but once you wear them, you're mated. She needs your protection. She doesn't think she does, but she does."

"What about the astral travel business?" Hunter asked. "That's what gets her into the most trouble."

"I'll work with her after dinner to share a technique that can help. But she'll have to practice at it."

Alana came out of the x-ray room all smiles. "Like with Celeste, the doctor did a great job setting my arm. I need to go to the cast room. Coming?"

"I'll see to our guests," Pappalios said, "and dinner. And a birthday party." He gave her a warm hug. Then he left and Hunter and Alana headed for the room where Celeste had gone.

"I'm glad you didn't have to have your arm rebroken. Come to think of it, Jared needs to have his ribs checked out."

Alana shook her head. "I forgot all about them. But he seemed to be able to help everyone just fine."

"Sometimes demons lie." Hunter escorted her into the casting room, and she took a seat to wait for her turn. "I'll be right back."

He headed to the living area and found everyone glued to the news. Picture after picture flashed across the screen of Alana and him rescuing people from the train car in peril, and the other that had crashed into the ravine. More pictures of everyone helping to organize supplies, Bentos taking charge, and even the small group of friends trying to rescue Celeste from beneath the train.

Witness statements were offered next, and Hunter shook his head. "I'm glad I don't live here permanently. I could see us being hounded by news reporters."

"They're already outside the gates," Pappalios said.

Then videos and photos showed the touching moment when Hunter unzipped his parka and pulled out a kitten to show Alana, the last one rescued from the train car wrecked below. And a picture of him handing the kitten over to the twelve-year-old, twin girls he'd rescued.

Most disturbing was seeing the crashing of the car on top of the other, the train bridge shaking, Alana falling, him falling, and her finally stopping their fall.

"Who was taking all these videos and photos? I thought everyone was helping," Hunter said.

"A historical documenter. She was in our car," Wendell said. "She's famous, an older woman, and unable to help much, except for documenting what happened, both for us to learn the truth, and for the train department to use for conducting its investigation of the accident. There are brief videos shot by passengers of the derailment. She would be providing those to the investigator's office."

Jared shook his head. "I didn't know how far you and Alana had dropped before she was able to regain her ability to levitate the two of you."

Pappalios let out his breath. "That is going to give me nightmares for ages."

"Hey," Hunter said to Jared. "You need to come with me."

"Yeah, sure. Are Alana and Celeste okay?"

"Yeah, no rebreaking their bones. They're getting casts right now." Hunter didn't want any of the others to know that he wanted Jared to have his ribs x-rayed.

When they arrived at the x-ray room, Hunter asked the technician, "Can you check out my friend? His ribs were bruised, maybe, but we need to make sure there aren't any breaks."

Jared looked resigned to do this.

"Sure, come in here."

Once the technician had taken the photographs and had the

radiologist look over them, he came to speak with Jared. "You have hairline cracks on two of your ribs. There's not much we can do for them. Within a couple of weeks, it should be healed."

"Could be up to six weeks if you were human," Hunter said.

"Want to sign my casts?" Celeste asked as she was wheeled out of the cast room.

"Yeah, me first," Jared said. "I...just need something to write with."

Hunter went in to watch as Alana's arm was cast.

"Did you mention anything about how someone might have hired a gate guardian to find Jared's parents?" Alana asked him.

"No, but I had them check his ribs. Two have hairline fractures."

"Oh, no. I'm so sorry."

"He'll be perfectly healed in a couple of weeks."

"Okay."

Her cast done, she held it up to Hunter. "Do the honors?"

Hunter glanced at the technician. She smiled and handed him a purple marker.

He frowned at it.

"Oh, do it. Purple's my favorite color," Alana said.

"You know I'm a Matusa, don't you?"

She laughed. "Yeah. Always."

He wrote in the biggest message he could: Mine. Love, Hunter

She laughed and wrapped her good arm around him. "I love you."

He wrapped his arms around her. "I love you right back. But my dad's sure to be a terror if we don't eat soon."

"What about you?"

"Me too."

She chuckled and they joined the others in the living area. He thought by now they would be watching something else, but it was just one news story after another, interviews from everyone they had saved, tears in two of the mothers' eyes whose babies he'd rescued. Video clips of him handing one of the babies to his father. Bentos looked horrified for a moment but then held the baby close to his chest for warmth and protection.

Bentos let out his breath in exasperation. "I will never be able to live this down."

Hunter laughed. Alana smiled.

"Are we ready to eat?" Bentos suddenly said, noticing Alana was done with her cast.

Wendell looked a little glum and said, "Hey, thanks for everything. I've got to run and see my parents. I should have before this, but…just thanks."

"I'll have my butler take you to their house in the loaner van," Pappalios said.

To everyone's astonishment, Wendell gave Celeste a hug and a kiss. "Thanks for saving me from the Matusa."

She looked even more surprised than everyone else.

Then the butler showed up and said, "This way, sir."

When Wendell and the butler left the house, Samson turned to Celeste, "Should I have socked him for kissing you like that?"

She only smiled, pulled a pink marker out of her pocket, and said, "Autograph?"

15

After dinner, and a special birthday cake created for Jared, promises of birthday presents when they returned home, everyone watched Demon Ninjas on TV, except Alana and her father. He was teaching her meditation skills in another room, relaxing music playing overhead, candles burning, the lights down low. He was trying to teach her how to block the pull of a portal while in mid-flight on an airplane, or at other untenable times.

She had closed her eyes while sitting on a pillow, hands resting on her knees, thinking of a blue, tranquil lake, birds tweeting and singing in nearby pine trees, and colorful monarch butterflies flittering about milkweed flowers. Meditating. Until she sensed Hunter leaning against the door jamb, watching her. She smiled.

"She's supposed to be concentrating on meditation," her dad told Hunter.

"She needs to learn to be able to control her astral travel even with distractions…like me, appear."

"She will. Eventually. She needs to practice at it."

Hunter began to jangle something in his pocket.

She ignored him. He jangled something again.

She frowned at him.

"Good, you're back for a moment. After all you've been through today, you need a break. Just to relax."

"No, I don't. This is much more relaxing than watching everyone rooting for their favorites in Demon Ninja. I need to learn how to do this." Then she patted the mat beside her. "Why don't you come join me?"

"The things I have to do for you." Hunter sat down next to her.

"The things I have to do for *you*!"

He pulled out the two gold rings from his pocket and placed one on her finger. Before he could place the other on his, she took it from him and did the honor. They glowed for a second.

"What does that mean?"

"It means that you're a matched pair," her dad said. "Wear them in good health. Now, I'll see if your friends want anything else while the two of you...meditate."

As soon as her dad left the room, Hunter pulled her onto his lap and kissed her mouth.

She smiled at him. "Now this is what I call...meditating."

He finally broke free of the kiss and frowned. "What was the business with the Matusa? Viton?"

"You were supposed to save me! But I had to save myself."

"Well, if you wouldn't keep appearing at portals."

"Which means I need to learn what my dad wants me to learn."

"We'll do it together. We'll make it a routine. And when you come back in the summer, you'll have it down pat by then."

Jared came running into the room. "We're famous! Well, you're famous! The two of you!"

"Now what?" Hunter asked.

"It's...it's all because of you. Three gate guardians heard the news about you and Alana saving all those people and how she's a gate guardian too. And they saw the one interview I gave where I was searching for where my parents had gone."

"Don't tell me they offered to search for them if you paid them," Alana said. "We would do it for free."

"No. I mean, yes, they're all doing it because of the news report. Because of what I did to help also. But they're doing it for free."

"The regent rulers will pay for it," Hunter said, smiling. "According to Alana's father."

"It doesn't matter. It means they'll help."

"Gate guardians. Why didn't your uncle call for a gate guardian to locate them when they disappeared?" Alana asked, getting off Hunter's lap.

He quickly joined her.

"He did. Miguel, one of the ones, looked, but he couldn't find them. For two years he looked. Whenever he's in that area, he looks. After learning that my parents had a son, who lost them, he's renewing his effort and calling others to help with the search. Isn't that great?"

"It is," Alana said. "It's great. But you know what? We have your fantastic demon trackers. I think now that we know the location where they first were, we have a good chance of locating them. If they're still in the area."

Pappalios returned to the room. "I say we work in teams. And I can help you with honing your skills at the same time, Alana."

Bentos cleared his throat at the doorway. "I'm willing to look for them."

"You're staying in Seplichus," Hunter said.

The way his father smiled so deviously at him, Hunter was sure he had an offer to make. And he suspected what it was. Learn who his half-brother was.

"Take me with you, and I'll show you your half-brother. *Show* you, *not* have you meet him. Not yet."

"That is *not* a good idea," Celeste said, Samson wheeling her into the room.

"You've had a vision?" Hunter asked.

"No. He's a Matusa!" Celeste smiled sweetly at Bentos.

"See your half-brother, or not. Your choice."

"What will you do to help us locate Jared's parents?" Alana asked, taking hold of Hunter's hand as if she didn't want him to make a mistake in bringing his dad with them.

"What if they are being held by an evil warlock summoner? Or a Matusa has enslaved them? Or Hunter is scratched by a Matusa again, and you need me to save his life? Besides, another pair of eyes might see something the rest of you are missing. But she"— Bentos waved his hand dismissively at Celeste—"will have to stay behind. She can't help like that."

"She will be partnered with you, and you can wheel her around," Hunter said.

"You know, I'm full Matusa, the one who is your father, and you should bow down to my will."

Hunter smiled. "You can't open a portal to go with us, so if you want to do this, you follow my rules."

"I'll go with Alana, to work with her on the astral travel business if that occurs while we're searching for them," her dad said.

Hunter slipped his arm around Alana. "I'll be with her too."

"Okay, so I guess that leaves you and me," Jared said to Samson.

Someone knocked at the front door as they were still deciding how they would do this.

"We'll return to the Hall of Records and leave from there. It's close to our hotel," Hunter said. "We were going to stay with Alana's uncle, but we couldn't reach him."

"I would like to meet him," Pappalios said.

"Me too," Bentos said, "since he's family." He glanced down at Hunter and Alana's rings. "You didn't have them on before dinner."

"It's official," Hunter said.

"I'll say it is," Bentos agreed.

"Sir," the butler said, "Wendell's back, and he has brought his parents. They want to personally thank everyone involved in saving Wendell's life and bringing him back to our world."

"Oh, yeah, sure," Celeste started to wheel herself out of the room, but Samson took hold of the wheelchair and pushed it for her.

Everyone left then to greet Wendell's family.

"Welcome," Pappalios said.

"Good to see you, Pappalios," the man said, shaking his hand.

"Thank you, Celeste, for putting yourself in danger when the Matusa tried to kill him." Wendell's mother gave Hunter and his father a worried look like she shouldn't have said anything bad about the Matusa in front of them.

"If there's anything we could do to thank all of you for bringing him home to us, anything at all, just let us know," his dad said.

Wendell said, "If you would like me to, Celeste, while you're gone, I'll keep searching the Hall of Records for any more of your family."

"I was only three when I was taken from my parents. I don't know their names or the name they would have called me even," Celeste said.

"How many Camaran parents would have lost a female child to a summoner around the time you were adopted?" Wendell asked.

"I guess that would narrow it down some."

"Wendell told us about your parents, and after we lost him, we know just how it feels. But you were just a baby. At least, we'd watched our son grow up. We all want to help you with this," Wendell's father said.

"But I have no idea where I was even summoned from or where I ended up. I was moved from foster family to foster family because of my psychic visions."

"We're Camaran demons like you. Your parents would be also. We have tons of family. We'll network with them, check the Hall of Records, and put out the word that we're looking for parents whose young daughter was taken when you were," Wendell's dad said.

"We will do everything we can," his mother agreed.

"You can stay with us and help if you would like," the dad said. "If we locate them, we'll want you to see them right away."

"We're going to look for Jared's parents in Earth world," Pappalios said. "But I'll return, and you can decide what you want to do at any time, Celeste. Stay here as long as you want to search for them, or return and finish out your school, then come back for the summer with Alana. Since you eat human food, you can always come here to eat. My home is open to you at all times."

"Can I eat here too?" Wendell asked, looking hopeful.

"Wendell," his mom scolded.

"Absolutely and you can keep Celeste company," Alana's dad said.

Jared smiled. "You've got to do it. Even if it doesn't work out, you've got to give it a shot. Staying here would be easier for you than running around all over the place from Dallas to Amarillo and who knows where else."

Celeste looked at Alana.

"Dad will take you to Baltimore to my mom's house when you're ready to return. I'll be there too, at the end of spring break, no matter what. I have to get my high school diploma," Alana said.

Samson agreed. "As long as they protect you, Celeste."

Celeste smiled.

Hunter said, "We'll see you one way or another. Good luck, Celeste."

Everyone wished her luck, and then Wendell wheeled her out to their van, and Samson hurried to help him load Celeste into the vehicle.

"Good luck to you also," Wendell and his parents said to Jared and the others.

"We'll miss you," Alana said, hugging Celeste. "If you find them and decide to stay here, that's your choice. Know that I will be visiting my dad during the year and will want to catch up with you. And if you want to return to our world, Dad will open a portal for you, or I will."

"Thanks, Alana. But I don't plan to stay."

"All right." Hunter wanted to get this show on the road. He knew things could change for Celeste when she finally found her parents—for good, or bad.

"Hey, you know we're getting so much publicity from the train wreck, as long as something else doesn't take over the news, maybe telling the reporter Celeste's story will help spread the word," Jared said.

"We'll get right on it," Wendell's dad said.

Then they said their goodbyes, and when they left, Pappalios said, "It's getting so late, why don't we stay the night and leave early tomorrow morning? After all that everyone's been through, I think a good night's sleep is in order. I have a bachelor pad for Hunter, Jared, and Samson, and your own kitchen for late-night snacks even. And Alana has her own room, next to mine. Bentos, you can take your pick of any of the remaining guest rooms."

Hunter had figured the rings meant he and Alana were married in the demon way, and he wanted to be with Alana tonight.

"After graduation," her dad said to Hunter as if he knew what Hunter was thinking.

Bentos was watching the exchange and laughed. Hunter was afraid he knew they weren't yet truly mated.

But Alana hugged Hunter and kissed him before she retired to her room.

Bentos stood next to Hunter as they watched Alana close her bedroom door, her dad retiring to a suite next to her room, and Jared and Samson checking out their new digs.

"Well, when you wear the rings, you're mated. Doesn't Alana know that?" Bentos asked Hunter.

"Not yet. But she will." Hunter smiled. He would tell her after they returned to her mother's home.

"You are a Matusa, even if you are half-human," Bentos reminded him. "But I'm proud of you." He slapped Hunter on the back and entered his room.

Hunter seriously considered telling Alana tonight. She would probably have a meltdown, and her dad would be angry with him. Better to wait until after they returned home. He retired to the bachelor pad that had one bedroom and a living area with two fold-out couches.

Wisely, Jared and Samson were busily making their beds on the sofas.

"What do you think will happen if we find your parents?" Samson asked Jared.

"No sense in speculating," Hunter said, walked into his bedroom, and shut the door.

"What Hunter said," Jared told Samson.

Hunter smiled. That's what he liked to hear. Complete agreement. Then he thought of Alana's stubbornness about waiting to be married until after college graduation. As much trouble as she had with staying in school because of her astral traveling misadventures, he couldn't wait for an eternity for her to graduate from college too.

Then he smirked. Until Alana could control the pull of a portal, he would see her.

He sat down on his bed and opened the portal.

Alana appeared in a pair of hearts, magic wands, and unicorn pajamas.

He grinned.

She folded her arms.

Alana's dad showed up too in a pair of black boxer shorts. He raised his brows.

Hunter quickly closed the portal and both Alana and her dad vanished. Well, *that* didn't work.

E arly the next morning, they all sat down to breakfast before they left for West where they would open a portal to Dallas. Alana smiled at Hunter, thoroughly tickled that he'd called not only her to the portal last night, but her dad. Hunter gave her a wicked smile back.

Her dad had said nothing about it, but she suspected he'd been more amused than anything, thwarting Hunter in his game. She knew Hunter wouldn't try that again while they stayed at her dad's place. Hunter had forgotten the part where her dad was a gate guardian too.

Bentos and her dad were talking about demon world politics.

"I swear that whole business of them failing to come for us any earlier than they did was a political mistake," Bentos said.

"I agree with you there." Her dad was eating eggs, bacon, and toast along with everyone else. "Heads will roll over that, especially since so much publicity came of it. And human-raised demons had to save so many lives. There's a public outcry about it already."

Bentos turned to Hunter and Alana. "Did Pappalios tell you? We have to make a quick stop in West to pick up a couple of medals."

"What?" Hunter said. "How long will *that* take?"

"Hopefully not long," Pappalios said. "The mayor was gratified to learn that you two have found your demon parents, but he wants to help both Jared and Celeste find theirs. Which could be a good thing. It means positive publicity for him and more help for us."

"But he can't go to Earth world to find them," Jared said.

"No, but he assumes Celeste's parents are still here. With learning that Treikal and a reigning prince are your distant relations, he wants to beef up the program wherein when our people go missing, there's more of a network to locate them. It's disorganized right now. We have to be born as gate guardians, so we can't just hire people to do the job. But he wants to have as many organizations assist us when we're trying to track down individuals."

"That's good news," Alana said. "We'll keep working in Earth world to send demons back whenever we can locate them."

"That's the other news." Her dad smiled. "From here on out, you'll be paid for your services."

"Demon currency won't help us in our world," Alana said, having rethought that scenario last night.

"Right. You're the only demon who works as a gate guardian in your world, so they're trying to devise a way in which we can convert the money."

"She can do that with her witch's skills, can't you?" Jared asked.

"No. No more than I can turn a metal object...or you...into gold."

"They're working on it, Alana," her dad said. "You'll get back pay for the ones we can verify were returned to their world, for both you and Hunter. They want you to do this full-time. No one knew a gate guardian could come about from the union between a gate guardian and a human."

"Okay."

"Of course, the witch part makes you even more special. I think they had the idea that gate guardians should try to create more, but that's not something that should be tampered with, I don't believe. You've had such a time dealing with this. It's not fair to you or your mother."

"I'm glad for what I am, but you're right. I'm sure not everyone could handle being part demon all that well. What if they turned out to be trouble?" Alana said.

Hunter looked at Bentos.

Bentos ignored his pointed look and continued to eat, but Alana knew Hunter was making an unspoken point about his half-brother. What if he turned out to be a bad Matusa, despite his human half? He could open a portal to the demon world at will, summon demons, and be worse than any summoner out there. Bentos had been fortunate that Hunter was one of the good guys.

"Is everyone ready?" her dad asked.

"Why, if you have so much money, don't you have a car of your own?" Alana asked her dad.

"I rarely use one. The train system is excellent here. Normally. But rest assured, I'll have one before you return in the summer."

"We can take the van loaned to us," Bentos said.

"Okay, let's go," Hunter said.

As soon as they reached the city of West, they were mobbed.

"Who told them we would be here?" Hunter asked, annoyed. They needed to take care of business, not be treated like celebrities.

A group of Matusa stood off to the side, their expressions growly, their arms folded across their chests. They didn't appear happy that a couple of Matusa had done good deeds and made such a name for themselves.

"We need—" Hunter said, as they were pushed toward a build-ing. "We need to take care of business."

A group of officious-looking demons made them go with

them, police officers keeping the crowds from grabbing at them further. Not at Bentos or Hunter, though. They might have proved they could do some good, but the lesser demons weren't so naïve to think that would pertain to them if they manhandled them.

They were led into an amphitheater filled with more officious-looking men and women, police officers at every exit.

"The mayor," Pappalios said, as they were escorted to the stage.

"Pappalios, we have a special seat for you here," a man said.

Hunter noticed that Wendell's parents and Celeste were there. Pappalios took a seat next to the dad.

A whole line of train passengers, who had helped others during the crisis, were seated on the side in a special box. Hunter and the others were directed to go there, but Alana and Hunter had reserved seats, even there.

The mayor talked for a good hour, and Hunter knew his eyes were glowing red. This was such a waste of time. Unless it helped Celeste to find her parents. He only hoped if she did, everything would be good between them.

Finally, the mayor finished his political talk and recipients for awards were called out. For all the help that Bentos had done with organizing everyone to take care of the injured and provide comfort for everyone else until a rescue, he was awarded a medal. He gave the mayor a dark smirk.

Hunter smiled. That was the highlight of this for him.

Then Alana and Hunter were called up together because they'd worked together and were given the highest award any demon could receive: the Medal of Valor.

He hoped they wouldn't have to give a speech next. But nope, the mayor spoke for another hour, captive audience, and then finally released them. There was to be a celebration later that afternoon. They thanked the mayor, said goodbye to Celeste and Wendell and his parents, had to wade through a bunch of thanks from passengers on the train, once again, and left the coliseum. They headed for the Hall of Records next door.

Once they were inside, Hunter hurried to open a portal. They all went through and ended up near their hotel room, where he shut the portal.

"All right, time to go to Amarillo," Hunter said.

"Ha! My Uncle Stephen and my mother left messages while we were away." Alana texted her mother, then called her uncle and put the call on speaker. "Uncle Stephen, we're back."

"Your mother was worried about you. She said you skipped your last two days of school to leave to see your dad early."

"Yes, we found a tortured demon and had to take him home. I won't tell you how we ended up getting demon Medals of Valor. But now we need to go to Amarillo because we've gotten word about where Jared's parents might be."

"It's only an hour's flight there," her uncle said. "Or six and a half hours if you drive."

"I sort of had a problem when I flew the last time."

"What happened?"

"I astral traveled from the plane. If a portal opens when I'm flying again—"

"I should be able to keep you safe," her dad said.

"What about a protective barrier? I could provide that," her uncle said.

"Are you going to come with us?"

"Yeah, you know I will," Uncle Stephen said.

"Were you at a conference?"

"Uh, not quite. I'm checking with one of my friends, and he said he can fly us out there. How many are we talking about?"

She told him.

"Okay, meet you at the airport in an hour."

"We'll be there."

"And you can tell me on the flight about the demon you rescued and took home. I take it you didn't have any trouble. But this business with you leaving school is a problem. If I have to, I'll home-school you so you can earn your diploma."

Jared was nodding. Samson was shaking his head.

Hunter knew her uncle was such a perfectionist, that he would drive her crazy.

"Uh, no, that's all right," Alana said. "I'll work extra hard to finish it on time."

"Okay, I have friends in Amarillo, and they can help us too. I'll let them know we're coming."

"Thanks, Uncle Stephen."

"See you soon."

When they ended the call, they piled into the rental car to head to the airport, and Jared drove them, though Bentos wanted to.

"You don't have a human driver's license, do you?" Hunter asked his dad.

"Sure I do. I see your half-brother and his mother here from time to time. She taught me how to drive, and I got my driver's license."

"Can you really stop me from astral traveling if it happens?" Alana asked her dad.

"Yeah. At least I think I can. I know what works for me. The first sign of a portal opening, and I sense it, I meditate. You'll have to practice at it like I told you before."

"Well, Uncle Stephen knows some barrier spells, and once he wrapped around me to prevent Hunter from calling to the portal."

Her dad glanced at Hunter. He only smiled.

"Okay, sounds like we've got the solution then," her dad said.

Hunter sat in the back seat with Alana, and she snuggled against him.

"You didn't open another portal in your bedroom last night," she said against his ear and smiled up at him.

He laughed. "I was trying to see if you could control the draw of the portal yet."

She shook her head. "You did not. You wanted to see me! Admit it."

He kissed her. "Yeah, but not your dad."

She chuckled.

"I should have known."

ON THE PRIVATE PLANE, Jared went into his storytelling mode to tell Alana's uncle everything that had happened, Samson nodding, while Alana and Hunter sat in seats in the back of the plane, cuddling.

"I don't think he'll ever get tired of telling that story," Hunter said to Alana, not wanting to hear it again. He, Alana, and their friends did what they had to do because that was their mission in life. Not to obtain awards for it. Then again, they were used to working "undercover," so to speak. In Earth world, no one could know what they were or what they did.

"At least, he doesn't embellish the story. Not that, as wild as it already was, there would be any need to," Alana said.

Suddenly, Hunter felt a frosty chill. "Indigo."

"Yeah, we missed you." She snuggled closer to Hunter to get warmer.

"Missssed you."

"How much do you want to bet, Jared will share this with his kids and grandkids someday," Hunter said, trying to ignore the ghostly Indigo.

"And about you saving his life."

"Ha! He saved my life by bringing you to me."

"I saved your life," Bentos said.

Hunter was amused because he wanted the credit. "Yes, but

only because Alana and Jared risked their safety by searching for you. And my mother had to summon you, which meant she also risked her life. But she was willing to so that she could save me."

Bentos snorted. "I would never kill her, though I was angry she gave you up for adoption when I thought she would raise you as her own child and love you. I didn't give you to her so she'd give you away."

Uncle Stephen glanced back at them. "You're wearing rings."

Bentos cast him a dark smirk. "They are mated so that Hunter can protect Alana from other Matusa who would covet a Kubiteron gate guardian."

Uncle Stephen's eyes widened. "I thought you were waiting."

"Until after I graduate." Alana smiled at her uncle.

Her dad cast Bentos an irritated look that told him to say no more of the matter.

Bentos only gave Pappalios a dark smile and winked at Hunter, as if telling him he had let the proverbial cat out of the bag, and Hunter could be with his mate now.

"Have you told your mother?" Uncle Stephen asked.

"Of course," Alana said.

Hunter knew she didn't realize still that they were mated now.

Uncle Stephen rubbed his beard in thought. "I thought you would stay with me and your dad at a wizard-owned hotel, but I guess you'll need your own suite with your mate."

Alana's jaw dropped. "Not until after graduation."

"But you're mated. And everyone agreed to give you their blessings," Uncle Stephen said.

She turned to her dad. "The rings are for pretend, just to show the Matusa that Hunter and I are together, right, Dad? That's why we're wearing them."

Benton chuckled.

Papplios looked like he could strangle Bentos. The Matusa had that effect on a lot of people.

Alana's eyes glowed red. Hunter loved it when they did. He couldn't help himself.

"Tell me you thought this was just a ploy until after I graduate from college," Alana said to Hunter, already pulling away from him.

"Alana, they would always come after you. I couldn't protect you always. Not unless I was your mate," Hunter said.

"I would protect her," Samson said.

"You knew!" She started to move to another seat on the plane, and Hunter held her hand for a moment as she glowered at him.

"I love you, Alana. And that will never change. It also means protecting you through whatever means are necessary."

"You were afraid I would find some cute college guy more to my liking."

Hunter smiled. No way did he think that.

She yanked her hand away from him and sat by Samson. "You can protect me." She patted him on the chest.

He puffed it out and leaned back against the seat, well-satisfied. "I will."

"Are you protecting her with your bubble?" Pappalios asked Stephen.

Samson quickly looked at Alana, as if worried she'd been pulled away, then breathed a sigh of relief.

"Yes. When she and Hunter were wrapped around each other, I had to do it around them, but now, just around Alana. Hunter doesn't need the protection."

Jared moved back to sit by Hunter. "You can protect me."

Hunter laughed. "You've got a deal."

17

When they landed at the airport in Amarillo, a limo van was waiting for them and took them to a hotel run by wizards.

Alana was still miffed with Hunter. Okay, so maybe she wouldn't go to college. Some fields of work needed more...hands-on experience. And the truth was, it was only two more months before she graduated from high school. As long as she graduated. She would just make Hunter suffer her indignation, except that he wasn't. He loved her, no matter how much she could be difficult about this. Which showed he was a demon.

Then again, she was too. "You're not off my list, buster," she said, sitting beside him in the limousine.

Uncle Stephen insisted they have their own rooms until they settled the differences between them.

After having a lunch of fajitas, they headed out in separate vehicles loaned to them, looking for demon signatures anywhere in the Amarillo area. Samson had one, so he paired up with Uncle Stephen. She gave hers to Bentos, who went with her dad.

Jared stuck with Hunter and her, and then they took off. Hunter was driving, Alana lying down in the back seat, her arm still hurting. She had Hunter's demon tracker, while Jared was sitting in the front seat, using his.

That was the role they played for four days—eating out, gathering at night at the wizard's hotel, searching all day long.

On the fifth day, they were all discouraged, assuming his parents were gone. That they had been moved to some other location. They didn't have a clue where else they could search for them, but they gave it one last shot.

"Behind us," Alana suddenly said.

"What? Oh, yeah, faint, some distance back. Elantus! Two Elantus!" Jared said. He was so excited.

She hoped he didn't get his hopes up too much. They could be anyone.

"Male and female!"

"Okay, turning around." Hunter got on Bluetooth. "Hey, we're on Main Street, and we picked up Elantus female and male signatures." He gave them the crossroad and the direction.

"On our way," Samson said.

Bentos agreed.

"They're splitting up," Jared said. "But I think they're on foot. Over there."

"And one is headed south," Alana said. "Pull the car over. I'm going after the one."

"I'll find the other," Jared said.

Hunter pulled the car into a parking spot in front of a craft store, then he joined Alana. Jared took off in the other direction.

Alana was directing them as they moved down an alley, onto the next street over, and then right again. "I swear the demon knows we're chasing him."

Hunter glanced at Alana. "Hell, they're Elantus demons. Maybe, if they're Jared's parents, they've designed something like he did."

Alana stopped and stared at Hunter. "Then they know we're after him, and he's probably afraid of you!"

"I'm not leaving you alone."

"Just for a few minutes. Stay here, and I'll be back for you."

"You've got my demon tracker. I can't even watch you to make sure you don't get into any trouble."

"I'll telepathically communicate with you." She quickly kissed him and took off in the direction the male was heading in. He'd raced into a bank, and she walked inside, nearly running into a man who was leaving the bank because she was watching the demon tracker.

The Elantus male had taken the elevator. She watched until the fourth-floor number was lit up. *"I'm at West Texas Bank, but just wait. He's gone up in an elevator to the fourth floor."*

"Be careful. I don't like this."

"They're Elantus."

"Yeah, and they can be as dangerous as any demon."

"All right." She raced up the stairs and when she reached the fourth floor, she saw the demon had entered the men's room.

Great.

She stood at the door. "We're looking for Elantus parents of a young boy that went missing nineteen years ago. I'm a gate guardian." She hoped only the Elantus was in the restroom. If anyone else was—

A man exited and smiled at her, then walked down the hall to an office. He walked inside and shut the door.

"Their boy is all grown up now, and he's desperately looking for his parents. His name is Jared. He doesn't remember his real name."

The Elantus male opened the restroom door. Man, did he look like an older version of Jared.

She wanted to hug him but smiled brightly instead. "You look just like Jared."

"Calamus."

"Uh, okay. Well, there are several of us here together searching for his parents, my dad and uncle, and my mate—"

Hunter strode toward them, and the man looked like he was having heart palpitations.

"That's my mate. Hunter, this is Jared's father."

Hunter smiled.

"He's half-human. You don't have to worry about him."

Bentos and Pappalios headed their way, and she quickly made introductions.

"I'm Pepe, Calamus's father." He looked shocked, like he was ready to collapse.

And then she saw the demon tracker in his hand and showed him hers. "Jared made them."

"We've been staying out of your range, figuring we needed to leave the city."

"Because of us?" Bentos asked.

"We figured the two Matusa were in charge of the others in some nefarious way, and they'd come for us."

"We actually saved a train load of passengers a few days ago in Seplichus," Bentos said, sounding proud of himself. "I might add, we were on our way to create a portal to enter Earth world where you'd disappeared to. But the train wreck prevented that."

"We left one of our friends back there to search for her parents," Alana said.

"Where's Samson?" Hunter asked his father.

"He took off after Jared."

Then Hunter got a call. "Yeah, Jared?" He put the call on speaker. "We found your father."

"I'm with my mom. She's crying and..." Jared was all choked up.

"Okay, why don't we all get together at Main Street where we left the vehicles and return to the hotel?" Hunter said. "They've got a sitting area we can go to and talk."

"You can come to our home," Pepe said.

"We'll follow them to their home," Hunter said then.

Samson said, "Jared and his mom will ride with me."

"All right."

Pepe gave them his address, and then they all left the bank to return to their vehicles and drive over to their home in the country.

"Now what happens?" Hunter asked Alana, as they followed Pepe to the house.

"I don't know. Your guess is as good as mine. They might want to return home now, but maybe not, if they know Jared's living here. Or they might all want to return. It's going to be hard on them to pick up the pieces no matter what. At least I think so. I feel like I've always known my dad."

"That connection, that bond we feel with someone who's family," Hunter said.

"Yeah, like you and Bentos." She knew it would be hard on Hunter if Jared left them. Not only because he was so good at making useful gadgets for them, but because he was a really good friend.

When they arrived at the country estate, Pepe invited them in.

Once they were all seated in the living room, Jared hugging his father, and then sitting between his parents on one of the sofas, they began to tell their stories.

"The summoner who brought us over had a heart attack. He was shocked to see that his birthday game had worked. So we were free of our summoner at least. But we had the problem with blending in with the human population, getting jobs, and a place to live. We both know so much about computers that we became programmers for a firm here in Amarillo. When Fern had the baby, Calamus, we were thrilled."

"I always thought I was born in Seplichus," Jared said.

"You were born here." His mother squeezed Jared's hand. "You were three when you were at pre-school, and someone picked you up and took off with you. They have better safeguards now, but at the time, they just didn't. The police looked for you for weeks. Your dad and I created our first demon trackers, but it took a week, and by then, you were long gone. We still searched for years, but we didn't hold out any hope that we would ever find you. And to think you had been searching for us all this time!"

Jared explained who everyone was in the group, and about Celeste and how she'd been injured, but was searching for her parents along with the Camaran demon she had saved.

"We're so proud of you," Pepe said.

Jared shook his head. "I never would have guessed you would have a tracker and would be watching our movement. It must have a longer range than ours, or we would have picked up your signatures."

"Ten miles out," his dad said.

Hunter looked at Jared. "Okay, so that's what *we* need."

Everyone smiled.

Jared said, "Well I'll just get my dad to make them."

"What are we going to do?" Jared's dad asked.

"Your brother was devastated to lose you. And I ran into Uncle Clyne on the train after we had the derailment. I'm sure all your family and friends would love to see you," Jared said.

"What about you? Would you live there?"

"No. I'm all grown up, and I have a job to do. I work with the gate guardians."

"Where's your home base?" Fern asked.

"In Baltimore. That's where Alana lives. Hunter and I live just down the street from her. Well, Celeste lives with her and her mother too. And Samson stays with us. Hunter and Alana can create a portal so I can return any time I want to see family."

"It wouldn't be enough," Fern said. "We want to see who you meet and marry. Be grandparents. We wouldn't want to be separated again."

"So you're saying you want to stay here?"

"Not here. Baltimore. I'm sure we can get jobs there, and then we would be close by. Not to tell you what to do, but to be there for when you want to see us, or just to talk," his dad said.

Jared smiled, looking relieved. "Okay, that sounds good. Our work takes us all over, but it would be nice to have the holidays together and visit whenever we can."

"What about your...other parents?" his dad asked.

"Ah, I love them, but they're absentee almost always. I've spent more Christmases with Hunter than anyone. Though this year, we planned to spend Christmas with Alana's mom."

"And Dad," Alana said.

Hunter looked at his own dad but didn't offer. Alana was sure he would spend it with his other son, and his wife.

"And any time you want to return to Seplichus, you would only just let us know," Hunter said.

"We would like to and see our families. To let them know we've lived here so long, and because of wanting to reconnect with Jared, we'll stay here," Pepe said.

"Okay, well, I can also open portals and am a gate guardian, so if you ever need me to help, just ask," Papplios said.

"We would like to see our family right away," Pepe said.

Fern nodded.

"We can arrange it."

And just like that the whole bunch made arrangements for the day, had dinner that night, and then the next morning, they flew back to Dallas. Uncle Stephen stayed there, but the rest would leave through the portal Hunter opened in his backyard.

"We'll be back," Alana said, hugging her uncle, "so I can finish school."

He smiled at her. "Good."

Then he shook Pepe's hand and smiled at Fern. Then each of them went through the swirling blue and green lights of the portal.

They were closest to Jared's uncle's house, so they went there first. The reunion between the brothers and Fern was heartwarming. A family celebration followed, with all of them included, since they'd been instrumental in locating Pepe and Fern.

But Alana couldn't wait to return to her dad's house, so she could get in touch with Celeste and see how her search was coming along. Jared was staying with his family. Hunter and his team would return, pick him and his parents up on the way back, and take them to Dallas.

As soon as they reached Pappalios's house, Alana wanted to take off to speak to Celeste, but Hunter and Samson felt the same way.

"Tell her I hope to see her soon," Alana's dad said.

"We will."

18

Celeste was worried about how her friends would feel about this whole business. She was a full Camaran demon and with her sense of adventure and her future visions, she had a job already lined up. No more having to go to a human school.

What could she hope to do as a pretend human? Alana was the one with good job prospects, and her mother lived with her too. Though Celeste knew Alana and Hunter would soon be a couple, and Celeste would be alone again. After meeting Wendell, and liking him and his parents, and them offering for her to live with them until she could locate her family, she realized she needed to stay here.

It hadn't taken them long to locate her parents in another city. Not when the media had been sharing her news for some time: how she'd saved the life of another Camaran demon in Earth world, nearly dying for her heroics. And how she and her friends had been in the train wreck that had made international news.

Her parents were certain she was their daughter and would have the DNA to prove it. She was glad for that because she worried

—what if this was just a lonely couple who wanted a daughter? Or maybe they wanted some of the fame?

Her parents had made the four-hour trip here to see her, and she had been excited and apprehensive at meeting them. What if they didn't get along? What if they set all kinds of rules for her? She had been on her own so much, she wasn't ready to be told what to do.

When they arrived, her mother, because she knew she was from the minute she laid eyes on her, burst into tears and hurried to hug her, as if they had never been apart. Celeste wished she wasn't wheelchair-bound at the moment. She knew, not only from the way her mother and she looked so similar, but she felt the familial connection right away. Her dad pulled her into a hug and the three wept, as her parents crouched on either side of her wheelchair.

Journalists had somehow learned of the meeting and flocked to capture the moment for the next news story. But she didn't care. She wanted other demons to know, who might have lost a family member to Earth world, that they should never lose hope, no matter how long it took.

After all the years of home placements, and not ever feeling at home anywhere, then finally meeting up with Alana and her friends, and Alana's mother taking her in, that had been the first real home she'd known.

But Pepe and Fern were her family. And here she could find more of her kind. Date. Mate. Fit in.

"You are so beautiful, Celeste," her mother said.

"You take after your mother," her dad agreed.

"I didn't think I would ever see you, and I didn't think we would feel this...bond," Celeste said, wiping away her tears.

"Always between family members, even distant ones," her mother said, glancing at the Camaran family smiling at the reunion.

"This is Wendell and his parents," Celeste said, "and they've put me up until we could find you. Though Alana's dad said I could visit there anytime. Pappalios is a gate guardian and lives a few houses down from here."

"We want to take you home with us, and well, you can decide what to do after that. We...we don't want to lose you again," her mom said.

"I'm of age," Celeste said, worried that they were going to keep a tight leash on her, afraid she would just vanish again. "I have a job offer with a leading group of psychics."

Her mom smiled. "Your dad and I started the organization."

"You knew?"

"Yeah, honey. We need a researcher, and we think you'll have our combined talents. You'll fit right in. The pay's excellent. You can live with us until you want to find a place of your own."

Celeste glanced back at Wendell. He was smiling. He must have known!

"You're an adult. No rules, Celeste. We're just so glad to have you back home."

"I might have half-human friends visit sometimes," Celeste said.

"Anytime."

"And I might return to Earth world to see them too. Alana's dad said he would help me get to Alana's mother's home. Alana's a gate guardian too."

"Absolutely," her mom said. "You have to know we gave up hope of ever seeing you again. When we saw all the news clips of those on the train and the one of you, we couldn't be certain it was you. Not until we started connecting the dots. That Alana and Hunter were half-human and had brought over human-raised demons to search for their families. You don't know how much we prayed that you were our missing baby daughter."

"Why don't we go inside and have something to eat?" Wendell's dad asked.

Wendell hurried to wheel Celeste into the house before her dad could. Her parents smiled at each other. Yeah, Celeste had her first boyfriend. Would he be the one for her like she knew Hunter was for Alana? Maybe not, but he would be her first real boyfriend.

She and Wendell had discussed how they had to locate Mikey, or Bengal, or whatever his real name was, and eliminate him. Their first "guardian" duty on this side of the world. He wasn't ever going to return to Earth world and hurt another demon again.

She was glad Wendell had just as much of a sense of adventure, though he'd asked if they could take along another Matusa to help even the odds. Hunter? She would ask.

But she didn't think they would get good publicity if everyone learned they were a vigilante group now too.

They would have to learn where Mikey had been left off in the demon world. He might have already left the area. It could take years to locate him. But they would find him.

Someone knocked on the front door, and Wendell's dad hurried to get it. "Probably the reporters wanting more news."

They all waited for him to come back to the table, but then they heard more footfalls than just his. Celeste couldn't believe he would bring reporters in to talk to them while they were eating dinner.

What shocked and thrilled her was that they weren't reporters, but her friends had returned, all but Jared. Her eyes were laden with tears again. She felt like a traitor for not wanting to return with Alana.

Alana smiled brightly at her and hurried to hug her. "We're so sorry to interrupt your meal. But we had to tell..." She looked at Celeste's mom and said, "Ohmigod, you found your parents!"

"This is Alana," Celeste said, then hurried to introduce every-one. "Where's Jared?"

"He found his parents. They're living in Amarillo, but they intend to move to Baltimore to be close to us and help with creating demon-tracking devices and other high-tech gadgets. They all came home to see family though."

"That's wonderful." Celeste still felt like a traitor.

"Now that you've found your family, what do you want to do?" Alana asked her.

"Stay here." She expected Alana to be upset with her, but all she did was smile again and give her another hug.

"But you'll visit sometime," Alana said as if it were a given.

"Join us for dinner, if you would," Wendell's dad said.

"Oh, we can't stay. Dad's fixing us dinner, and we're leaving first thing tomorrow. But we just wanted to share the good news about Jared, and we're thrilled about your good news too."

"Do you mind wheeling me out to the back porch so we can talk for a moment?"

"Sure, just tell me the way."

Everyone began talking about what Hunter and Samson did in Earth world as they helped other demons, and they were glad to give Celeste and Alana a moment alone together.

When they were on the back porch, and Alana had shut the door, Alana asked, "This is what you want?"

"Yes, more than anything. It's not the same for you and the others. They have a family they love in Earth world. I have all of you, but my family is here."

"And a boyfriend," Alana said, smiling.

"Maybe not as much of a sure thing as you and Hunter, but time will tell. I hate to abandon you and then have to ask you a favor."

"We will be sisters, always." Alana sat on the step next to her. "You can ask me anything."

"Wendell and I want to kill Mikey, Bengal, or whoever he is. After he nearly murdered the two of us, he doesn't deserve to live. What if he returns to Earth world? What if he does this to demons in this world?"

Alana nodded. "We would have to learn where he ended up in Seplichus."

"Right."

"He might have left the area."

"True. Why didn't you just kill him after what he did?"

"Anna was a witness. Hunter wanted her to believe that Mikey was a real demon and tell her friends how dangerous he was. If he'd killed him, she would have thought Hunter was the danger, the demon, as Mikey had said."

Celeste frowned. "Omigod, what if Mikey's seen the news about us? He would know where we are. That your dad is a gate guardian? What if he tried to force him to send him back to kill you and Hunter? Me, for not dying? Wendell, the same thing."

Alana opened her mouth to speak, then clamped it shut. "We need to tell the world who he was, what he looked like, how evil he is. The people here will try him. We'll have to return to the abandoned house and learn where the portal went through to the demon world, and then we can give that information to my father. He can spread the word."

"All right. I guess that's the best idea. Especially since I can't walk for a while."

"But we need to warn your family and friends of the danger you and Wendell could be in, that any of them could be in for being close to you."

"Okay. We...we thought we could just ask Hunter if he could help us kill him and that would be the end of it. But I can see how this could go sideways. Are you sure you're not upset with me for staying here?"

"I'm so happy for you."

"My parents have a psychic research facility, and I have an important job there."

Alana smiled. "We only wanted you to be happy wherever you are."

"I guess we should go back and tell them the news about Mikey."

When they returned to the dining room, Hunter looked glad to see Alana was fine. Celeste wanted a mate like that.

She explained about Mikey, aka Bengal, and how dangerous he was.

Wendell was frowning at her like he wished they had taken care of it on their own. But they couldn't. Not when the guy was a Matusa demon. And not when he could hurt any of their family or friends.

"We'll take care of it," Hunter said.

Alana raised her brows at him.

"I should have killed him when I had the chance."

"Learn where he ended up in Seplichus, and we'll make sure he has a warm welcoming committee," Celeste's dad said. "Attempted murderers don't have any place in our society."

"Agreed," Wendell's dad said.

"Okay, well, we've got to run. I'm so happy for you, Celeste, and when I come this summer, I'll be sure to visit you," Alana said.

"Me too," Hunter said, "since she's not going anywhere without me." He held up his ring, just to let Celeste's parents know they were mated.

"Me too," Samson said.

Nobody had invited him for the summer, but Celeste expected where Alana went, Samson and Hunter went. She wondered about Jared now too.

They said their goodbyes and Wendell's dad saw them out. "You don't have to do this alone. Everyone will help you with this. I know that look in your eye."

Hunter grunted. "I wanted to keep the other students from following in the same footsteps as Mikey. But I did Celeste and Wendell a great disservice by allowing the demon to live. I always correct my mistakes. Always."

"You don't have to do this alone. You'll have a ton of people at your back. Let us know when you find him. *Please*."

Hunter gave him a stiff nod, but Alana knew that look. Hunter had to fix his mistake, and she prayed he wouldn't get himself killed doing it.

"When do we find him?" Samson asked.

"You're to protect Alana at all times," Hunter told him, as they headed back to Alana's dad's estate.

"No way. We stick together."

Hunter scowled at him. "You always say you're Alana's protector. Now you're mine? I'm a Matusa!"

Samson smiled, then frowned. "And you're bound to get yourself killed."

When they returned to her dad's house, Alana told him what had happened. He was thrilled that Celeste had found her family, but not happy at all about the business with Mikey. Bentos was quiet, taking it all in. Alana thought he would believe it was Hunter's job to do just as he said he would do.

"You tell me where he is in our world, and I'll go after him," Bentos finally said. "Your job is to take care of those who are in Earth world."

"Your job isn't to take care of them in this world."

"He went after your friends. He's bound to go after you and Alana. You're family. Family protects family."

Hunter let out his breath as they sat down to eat a dinner of steak, potatoes, and spinach. Her dad hadn't lied about loving steak. "Okay, look, I'll open a portal, and see where it leads to. But if he's in the vicinity, I won't have time to return to Earth world, to fly to Dallas, to come here, and seek you out with the news."

Bentos smiled. "That works for me. I'll go with you."

"Back to Baltimore?"

"That's where my wife and son are. Do you want to meet

Rolling? I'll show him to you. But we'll take care of this other business first."

"That's a deal," Alana said. Hunter had wanted to see his half-brother. And she wanted Hunter to have backup against Mikey. Who knew what powers he might possess?

HUNTER COULDN'T BELIEVE his dad was negotiating with him, wanting to fight his battles, and his mate was siding with his father.

"And, we can be mates, now," Alana said, holding onto Hunter's arm, leaning over to kiss his cheek.

He smiled darkly. Now *she* was good at negotiations. "It's a deal."

"Jared should have been here to see this," Samson said, chowing down on the steak.

"I'm going with you," Pappalios said. "To see my wife and protect Alana."

"You know, I was thinking, I need to get Uncle Stephen to teach me how to create a barrier spell like he does, to keep me from being pulled to a portal," Alana said.

"Can you learn it?" Hunter asked.

"Not all spells. It's like some are good at math, others great at computer technology, some at artwork, we never know which skills we can learn unless we try. And then of course tons of practice has to go into it too."

"Well, let's ask him when we get back there."

After dinner, they packed their bags and discussed what they would do. They planned to pick up Uncle Stephen so that he could work on the barrier spell with Alana while also visiting with her dad and mother. In the meantime, they needed to tell Jared what they planned to do.

Then everyone peeled off to their rooms except Alana and Hunter.

They were settled on the couch, and he had his arm wrapped around her. "You know it's still your choice. After graduation, we can be mated."

"College?" she asked, lifting her brows.

He smiled. "No, high school. And that's only if you graduate on time."

"I promised to be mated to you now. Unless you've changed your mind?"

Hunter chuckled darkly. "Never." He lifted her off the couch and carried her to her bedroom. "This has been too long in coming." Then he carried her into the bedroom, shut the door with his hip, and set her down on her bed.

"You are—"

"Beautiful," she finished for him, pulling off his shirt. "And you are—"

"Hot."

She laughed. "True. I was going to say you were mine before you said it and irritated me."

He chuckled. They were soon in bed, loving each other as a mated couple should, and he thought he would never be mating his lovely Kubiteron in a bed in the demon world—in her dad's home, no less.

Alana couldn't have loved Hunter more. She so appreciated that though she'd made the offer to be his mate now and forever, he'd still given her the option to wait until...well, the graduation date he was still calling for. Not that she could have waited through college either.

No more calling her via a portal to stoke her ire. Though she hoped to get that under control soon too.

She wondered why she'd put this off for so long. She loved Hunter as much as he loved her.

19

The next day, they finally arrived back in Baltimore. Alana's mom was thrilled to see Pappalios and Alana return safely. She was happy to see her brother too. Uncle Stephen had been telling Alana the spell over and over again on the flight from Dallas to Baltimore to protect herself from a portal call. But she didn't know if his protection worked, or if they just hadn't run into any portals opening on the earth below them during the trip.

Jared had been talking away to Samson in the seat behind them on the plane. His parents had stayed behind to visit for a couple of weeks with family. But Jared had to help Hunter on this mission. Pappalios would open a portal to Dallas when Jared's family wanted to return there.

For now, they would unpack and settle in before they headed over to the abandoned house out in the country, to see where they ended up.

Bentos left to visit with his wife and son, promising that Hunter would see his half-brother after they took care of Mikey.

"He'll take you to him," Alana said, squeezing Hunter's hand.

"Hopefully the kid is more like me than my father," Hunter said.

Alana's mom smiled at them. "I hear you're properly mated."

"Yeah, we're going to Hunter's apartment tonight," Alana's said. Jared cleared his throat.

"Well, technically Jared's apartment," she added.

"And Celeste is finally home. I'll miss her," her mom said.

"We all will, but she'll return."

RIGHT AFTER LUNCH, Bentos returned to the house. "Ready to scout out the demon world?"

"Yeah, I sure am," Hunter said.

"I'm going with you," Alana said.

"You were supposed to stay here with your uncle and dad and mom," Hunter said, frowning.

"If he's a fire demon, you can use my help."

"We can all go. Except for your mom. She stays home," Pappalios said.

Alana was glad for that. Her mother dealt with some nasty poltergeists. She didn't need to face demons too.

"Let's go."

They took Jared's Jeep and Hunter's truck.

Bentos and her dad sat in the back seat of Hunter's truck, while Hunter drove, and she navigated, in case he'd forgotten where the house was located.

Jared followed behind them with Samson and Uncle Stephen.

When they reached the site, they saw a group of teens gathered, wearing black cloaks that looked like they'd picked up black graduation gowns early.

"Omigod, he's back," Alana said, "and he's casting a fireball this way!

Someone in his little demonic group of so-called hunters must have used a summoning spell he'd given them and called him right back.

"We'll take care of him and anyone else who wants to join him," Bentos said, his voice filled with dark purpose.

Hunter tore off of the dirt road, trying to avoid the fireball hitting his pickup.

Alana was conjuring a water spell to put it out, afraid the blast would hit Jared's Jeep before he was aware it was coming when Hunter moved out of its path.

He didn't have time to turn the Jeep, and Samson and Jared jumped from the vehicle. Her spell helped to reduce some of the fireball, but she couldn't put it out.

Uncle Stephen was working some kind of a reverse spell and sent the fireball back to the Matusa. But he was a fire demon. He couldn't be hurt by the fire.

Alana figured her spell wasn't as effective through the glass windows of the truck. She and the others scrambled to get out of the truck.

Fourteen or fifteen kids standing around Mikey, wearing black robes and carrying scythes, scattered as the fireball headed back in Mikey's direction. They thought their demon was all-powerful, but they didn't know who they were messing with.

Mikey threw a new fireball but held it in place and spread the fire out into a wave. Then he hurdled it toward them. But it moved slowly.

Hunter was working on his heart-stopping spell on the demon. Maybe that was slowing the Matusa down a bit.

Three of the teens came at them with the scythes. They had to be brainwashed or crazy.

Alana was working on a wall of water to protect her team from the wave of fire. Her arm was killing her with the strain, and she'd never cast a spell where she had to spread the wall so far out.

Her dad opened a portal in front of the three kids, and suddenly they were falling inside. She wondered if Jared was invisible and had anything to do with it. Her dad quickly closed the portal.

Her uncle cast a lightning bolt at Mikey, who held his hands high, trying to stop the electrical charges from striking him.

The other kids stood watching, afraid to move.

Hunter was concentrating on his heart attack spell, constricting the blood vessels to the demon's heart. It took a little time though, and the demon was still pushing the fire against her wall barrier.

Jared and Samson had vanished.

Jared could turn invisible, and Samson could turn into mist. She hoped they were taking care of the kids. This time, she would wipe their minds completely of all this business.

But they would have to take care of the ones who went to the demon world also. If they could summon a portal, they could still be real trouble.

The fire began to break through her wall. One section hit the abandoned house, and it began to burn. Another fire ball broke through and headed for Jared's Jeep. The Matusa was strong.

She couldn't hold the fire back and she couldn't put it out.

"Make a rain spell, Alana," her uncle shouted. "He's using some kind of barrier spell against my lightning bolts."

Rain wouldn't put out the fire that quickly, she didn't think. She had to let go of her water wall spell and feared they were all doomed. The fire broke through as soon as her water wall was down. Immediately, she cast a torrential rain spell. It was only a trickle at first, and she kept forcing more rain to appear until it was a soaker. But it only extended from right before the path of the fire and back to the demon, hoping to stop him if he tried any new fireball spells.

It was dampening the fire, sending steam up, making it hard to see the demon in the mist. And then she realized Hunter was standing in the middle of a section of fire. Her jaw dropped. He wasn't burning. He was still working on the heart attack spell, and he looked in his element.

Her uncle cast a lightning bolt at the demon again. This time the demon's face was red with exertion, and he tried to keep her uncle's lightning bolt from breaking through his barrier.

Mikey suddenly clutched his chest, and Alana knew Hunter's spell was close to killing him.

The lightning bolt struck the Matusa and because he was sopping wet and was standing in water, the electricity continued to zap him. He collapsed on the ground, his face ashen, his hair standing out like he'd been hit by a million volts of electricity.

Alana continued with her rain spell until the fires had burned out. Steam filled the whole area. She turned her rain on the abandoned house until she could put the fire out there and on the surrounding meadow grasses.

Hunter watched the Matusa for any signs of life, though he didn't approach him until the electrical charges died out.

Bentos stood there with his arms folded across his chest. "Here I thought I had a role to play."

"Why didn't you do something?" Hunter asked.

Jared and Samson appeared next to him.

"He did," Jared said. "He helped round up all the witless kids involved in this. They're all tied up in the barn over there."

"We've got to get the others in case they can summon a portal," Pappalios said. He opened a portal and hurried through it.

Bentos went with him.

Uncle Stephen glanced at Alana. "I've got this, Uncle Stephen. Go help the others."

The electrical charges had stopped, and Hunter went to check on Mikey.

Alana was *still* trying to put out all the fires. As soon as she'd thought they were all out, she heard crackling in a new area.

Hunter was cautious, not trusting that the demon was truly dead.

The guy was staring up at him, his hair standing on end, his face contorted in pain, his hands clutching his chest, but he wasn't dead.

Hunter extended claws. After a Matusa poisoned him in such a painful way, he didn't think he would ever resort to such a tactic. But it was fatal, unless another Matusa had the antibody to save the infected Dark One. Hunter clawed the Matusa across the chest.

"You're...not...a hero. You're...just...a...killer...like...me," Mikey spit out.

"Hardly." Hunter watched the demon's face turn bright red with fever, the scratch marks sending red streaks up his chest toward his throat and then to his face. Hunter had been able to fight off his infection for a while, partly with Alana's healing help, but this demon was already too weak to battle it.

Mikey would never form another group of demon hunters like this again. Shortly, he would die.

Fifteen minutes later, he *was* dead. An hour later, Bentos and the others finally rounded up the other kids who were hiding in various areas in Seplichus, terrified that demons were ready to kill them for invading their world. They'd also taken Mikey's dead body back to the demon world.

Alana had finished putting out fires and was busy wiping the kids' minds of the demon business.

"When you return home, Dad, can you let Celeste and Wendell know that Mikey has been taken care of?" she asked.

"You know it."

"What do we do with them?" Bentos asked.

"I'm sending them to the police station to admit to starting the fires on the two abandoned homes, and this whole area. They can take their scythes with them and try to explain why they're dressed as devil worshippers. They won't remember what happened here otherwise." Alana glanced at Hunter. "You poisoned Mikey?"

"Yeah. Fitting end."

"Ready to see your half-brother?" Bentos asked.

Hunter nodded. "It's time."

Alana told the kids to go straight to the nearest police station. They hurried to get into vehicles parked on the other side of the barn and tore off.

Jared and Samson returned to their apartment to get cleaned up. They dropped Stephen and Pappalios off at Alana's mother's home. Bentos, Hunter, and Alana went to see Hunter's half-brother.

She couldn't believe Bentos's family was in the same city as she was. Then again, Hunter had been living in Dallas.

They saw a sixteen-year-old boy practicing martial arts with another boy. If that didn't make her think of Hunter and how he was always practicing with Jared. The one boy was a Matusa who looked similar to Hunter. The other was a warlock.

Alana grabbed Hunter's arm, and whispered, "Matusa and warlock."

Both boys turned to look at them.

"Dad," the one boy said, then gave Alana a big smile.

She rolled her eyes, but Hunter tucked her under his arm. He would never have thought his little half-brother would be interested in his mate. He should have known better.

"Well, who have we here?" the boy asked, coming to join them.

Bentos said, "Your famous brother, Hunter, and his mate, Alana. This is Rolling."

Rolling looked down at their rings and lost his smile.

"And your friend?" Alana asked, her brows furrowed.

"Everett."

"A warlock," she said.

"Takes a witch to know a warlock," Everett said.

"She's much more than that." But Rolling didn't elaborate any further. "So what do I do with a half-brother?"

Bentos sighed. "You learn from him. Maybe someday you will be as great as him and his mate."

Hunter smiled. "I will be happy to show you the ropes." But then he frowned. "Only if you want to do right."

"Rolling," a woman called out from inside a two-story, blue house. "Rolling! Did you take out the garbage yet?"

"I will. I will."

Hunter chuckled, remembering a time when his human mother was always after him to take out the garbage when he was so intent on saving the world.

"I look forward to getting to know you," Hunter said.

"Your brother and his 'mate' are intense." Everett headed into the house with Rolling.

"I think life is about to get interesting," Rolling said.

Hunter just hoped he didn't get his kid brother killed, but he'd been only thirteen when he'd started hunting demons. His brother was an old man by his standards. He would have a lot of catching up to do.

"Are you staying, Dad?" Hunter asked.

"Yeah. I'll see you later."

"Thanks for your help out there."

"Thanks for being my son."

Hunter opened the truck door for Alana and helped her onto the seat. She looked worn out. "I didn't think my brother would have the hots for my mate."

She laughed. "I guess tomorrow's another day of school. I'm going to miss Celeste."

"She wasn't at school half the time."

"Is Jared going to quit now?"

"No. It's still you, me, Jared, and Samson against the world."

"And Indigo."

"Don't mention it."

"I think your brother seemed nice."

"Did you see the look he gave me? He's itching to prove he's more powerful than me." Hunter drove off to Jared's apartment.

"He might be, depending on the skills he has. I would watch out for the warlock too. Between the two of them, you'll have your hands full."

"Aren't you going to help me?"

She smiled. "I'll sit back and watch. I'll learn their strengths and weaknesses first."

"That's all in a day's work for us."

Two weeks later at school, Alana saw Anna, the former demon hunter, but this time, Anna was just going to classes, complaining about the crappy nail polish she was wearing to another girl. She wasn't with any of the other demon hunters. Good, Alana's mind wipe had worked.

Indigo was doing his ghostly artwork on the board before the teacher arrived. Alana never got to class this early, but she was determined to graduate from school on time.

Samson hurried to join her. "Where's Hunter? You're not supposed to be alone."

"He's checking out some of the former demon hunters, making sure none of them remember anything. Jared's with him too."

"Okay, I've got your back then." Samson seemed proud he still got to be her guard when Hunter wasn't there to watch over her.

What shocked her to the core was when Celeste and Wendell rushed into class.

"Celeste! Wendell!" Alana jumped up from her desk, glad to see the two of them. Celeste was no longer wearing casts, just like

Alana was free of hers. "What are you both doing here?" She gave them both a hug.

"We had a vision," Celeste said. "A summoner is at the zoo."

"Again? Oh, no, oh, no." Alana tried to meditate, tried to place a barrier around her but all she heard was Samson calling on his phone right before she...astral traveled.

"Alana's gone. Celeste and Wendell say the summoner is at the zoo."

"Celeste and Wendell?" Hunter said, rushing with Jared back to the classroom.

The team was back together again, well, with the addition of Wendell.

The teacher walked into the room.

Hunter swept Alana into his arms. "She's having another episode."

And then he and the others headed out of the school to their vehicles. "To the zoo."

And more summoner trouble.

"What did you see?" Hunter asked Celeste and Wendell as he drove toward the zoo.

"Alana's in the lion pit," Celeste said.

"Lion pit?" Hunter drove faster. Neither Alana's meditation spells nor any barrier she'd tried to erect, had stopped her from being pulled to a portal.

They had to come up with something else.

For now, he was going to kill a summoner and rescue his mate from a lion. He glanced at the time. The zoo wasn't even open yet. *Great.*

ALANA COULDN'T BELIEVE she was in a lion's den, of all places. If she had to, she would summon a portal and jump into the demon world, but she didn't want to do anything that drastic, except as a last resort. She was sitting up at the top of the cliffs, just where the lionesses liked to gather. She knew because every time she'd come to the zoo, this was where they would rest, observing the humans watching them.

Luckily, the two lionesses and one lion hadn't seen her yet as they were sprawled out down below.

"Alana, we're on our way. Celeste and Wendell told us where you are. Whatever you do, don't climb to the top of the cliffs. The lionesses will be headed there any minute. Are you okay?"

"No. I'm at the top of the cliffs, which is where I landed. But one of the lionesses just saw me. She's trying to figure out what I am. Now she's coming. The other looked up to see what she saw. She's joining her. I can levitate myself away from the cliff. But hurry. I don't want any zoo official to see me."

"Okay. We're almost there. Parking. Running."

"Story of my life, Hunter."

"Love you, Alana."

"Love you, Hunter. Always."

The lionesses took several leaping bounds, and Alana levitated herself away from the ledge. A fence covered the top of the enclosure, so she couldn't go that way. The lion was standing now, watching to see if she would come down for dinner.

"Hurry, Hunter!"

And that's how their lives would always be. One big, dangerous adventure. Just like they liked it. Well...usually.

And the team, plus one, was together again.

The End

IF YOU'RE LOOKING for another YA book filled with danger, intrigue, mystery, and a little romance, check out The Dark Fae!

ABOUT THE AUTHOR

Bestselling and award-winning author Terry Spear has written over a hundred romance novels. Her first werewolf romance, *Heart of the Wolf*, was named a 2008 *Publishers Weekly's* Best Book of the Year, and her subsequent titles have garnered high praise and hit several *USA Today* bestseller lists. A retired officer of the U.S. Army Reserves, Terry lives in Spring, Texas, where she is working on her next wolf, jaguar, cougar, and bear shifter romances, continuing with her Highland medieval romances, and having fun with her young adult novels. When she's not writing, she's photographing everything that catches her eye, making teddy bears, and playing with her Havanese puppies and grandchildren. For more information, please visit www.terryspear.com, or follow her on Twitter, @TerrySpear. She is also on Facebook at http://www.facebook.com/terry.spear. And on Wordpress at: Terry Spear's Shifters http://terryspear.wordpress.com/

AFTERWORD

Note to Reader:

Thanks so much for reading my Demon Guardian Series!! I hope you have enjoyed the demon guardians as they and all the trouble they get into!

Terry Spear

http://terryspear.wordpress.com/

ALSO BY TERRY SPEAR

Adult Titles

Romantic Suspense: Deadly Fortunes, In the Dead of the Night, Relative Danger, Bound by Danger

***

The Highlanders Series: His Wild Highland Lass (novella), Vexing the Highlander (novella), Winning the Highlander's Heart, The Accidental Highland Hero, Highland Rake, Taming the Wild Highlander, The Highlander, Her Highland Hero, The Viking's Highland Lass, My Highlander

Other historical romances: Lady Caroline & the Egotistical Earl, A Ghost of a Chance at Love

***

Heart of the Wolf Series: Heart of the Wolf, Destiny of the Wolf, To Tempt the Wolf, Legend of the White Wolf, Seduced by the Wolf, Wolf Fever, Heart of the Highland Wolf, Dreaming of the Wolf, A SEAL in Wolf's Clothing, A Howl for a Highlander, A Highland Werewolf Wedding, A SEAL Wolf Christmas, Silence of the Wolf, Hero of a Highland Wolf, A Highland Wolf Christmas; SEAL Wolf Hunting; A Silver Wolf Christmas, SEAL Wolf in Too Deep, Alpha Wolf Need Not Apply, Between a Wolf and a Hard Place, SEAL Wolf Undercover, Dreaming of a White Wolf Christmas, Flight of the White Wolf, All's Fair in Love and Wolf, A Billionaire Wolf for Christmas, SEAL Wolf Surrender, Silver Town Wolf: Home for the Holidays, Night of the Billionaire Wolf, You Had Me at Wolf, Joy to the Wolves, The Wolf Wore Plaid, Jingle Bell Wolf, The Best of Both Wolves, While the Wolf's Away, Christmas Wolf Surprise, Wolf Takes the Lead, Wolf on the Wild Side, Her Wolf for the Holidays, A Good Wolf is

Hard to Find (2024), Dreaming of a Highland Wolf (2024), Wolf Bound, Mated for Christmas (2024) , The Wolf of My Eye

SEAL Wolves: To Tempt the Wolf, A SEAL in Wolf's Clothing, A SEAL Wolf Christmas; SEAL Wolf Hunting, A SEAL Wolf in Too Deep, SEAL Wolf Undercover, SEAL Wolf Surrender

Silver Town Wolves: Destiny of the Wolf, Wolf Fever, Dreaming of the Wolf, Silence of the Wolf; A Silver Wolf Christmas, Between a Wolf and a Hard Place, Home for the Holidays, Jingle Bell Wolf

Wolff Family Lodge Wolves: You Had Me at Wolf, Wolf on the Wild Side, A Good Wolf is Hard to Find

Highland Wolves: Heart of the Highland Wolf, A Howl for a Highlander, A Highland Werewolf Wedding, Hero of a Highland Wolf, A Highland Wolf Christmas, The Wolf Wore Plaid, Her Wolf for the Holidays, Dreaming of a Highland Wolf, The Wolf of My Eye

Billionaire Wolf Series: A Billionaire in Wolf's Clothing, A Billionaire Wolf for Christmas, Night of the Billionaire Wolf, Wolf Takes the Lead

White Wolf Series: Legend of the White Wolf, Dreaming of a White Wolf Christmas, Flight of the White Wolf, While the Wolf's Away, Mated for Christmas

Red Wolf Series: Seduced by the Wolf, Joy to the Wolves, The Best of Both Wolves, Christmas Wolf Surprise

Greystoke Wolf Pack: Wolf Bound

Wolf Novellas: Day of the Wolf, Seal Wolf Pursuit, Wolf to the Rescue, Night of the Wolf, United Shifter Force

***

Heart of the Jaguar Series: Savage Hunger, Jaguar Fever, Jaguar Hunt, Jaguar Pride, A Very Jaguar Christmas, You Had Me at Jaguar, The Witch and the Jaguar, Dawn of the Jaguar

***

Heart of the Cougar Series: Cougar's Mate, Call of the Cougar, Taming the Wild Cougar, Covert Cougar Christmas, a novella, Double Cougar Trouble, Cougar Undercover, Cougar Magic, Cougar Halloween Mischief, Falling for the Cougar, Cougar Christmas Calamity, Catch the Cougar (Halloween Novella), You Had Me at Cougar, Saving the White Cougar, Big Cat Magic

***

White Bear Series: Loving the White Bear, Claiming the White Bear, Bear of a Halloween

Grizzly Bear Series: Bear in Mind

***

Wolves of Old: Wolf Pack, Wolf Alliance, Wolf Heir

Heart of the Huntress Series: Killing the Bloodlust, Deadly Liaisons, Huntress for Hire, Forbidden Love, Deadly Liaisons, Vampire Redemption, Primal Desire, Huntress Unleashed

Vampire Novellas: The Siren's Lure, Vampiric Calling, Seducing the Huntress

***

Comedy Romance: Exchanging Grooms, Marriage, Las Vegas Style

***

Science Fiction: Galaxy Warrior

Young Adult Titles

The World of Fae:

The Dark Fae

The Deadly Fae

The Winged Fae

The Ancient Fae

Dragon Fae

Hawk Fae

Phantom Fae

Golden Fae

Falcon Fae

Woodland Fae

Angel Fae

***

The World of Elf:

The Shadow Elf

The Darkland Elf

Warrior Elf

***

Blood Moon Series:

Kiss of the Vampire

Bite of the Vampire

Night of the Vampire

The Vampire Chronicles Series:

The Vampire in My Dreams

Demon Guardian Series:

The Trouble with Demons

Demon Trouble, Too

Demon Hunter

Non-Series for Now:

Ghostly Liaisons

The Beast Within

Courtly Masquerade

Deidre's Secret

The Magic of Inherian:

The Scepter of Salvation

The Mage of Monrovia

Emerald Isle of Mists